# Music to her Heart

# Music to her Heart

Jillian Dagg

Black Lyon Publishing, LLC

**MUSIC TO HER HEART**
Copyright © 2014 by Jillian Dagg

Our books may be ordered through your local
bookstore or by visiting the publisher:

**BlackLyonPublishing.com**

Black Lyon Publishing, LLC
PO Box 567
Baker City, OR 97814

This is a work of fiction. All of the characters, names,
events, organizations and conversations in this
novel are either the products of the author's vivid
imagination or are used in a fictitious way for the
purposes of this story.

ISBN-10:    1-934912-66-2
ISBN-13:  978-1-934912-66-9
Library of Congress Control Number:  2014938376

Published and printed in
the United States of America

**Black Lyon Contemporary Romance**

*In memory of Betty & Donald McCrady.*

# Chapter One

Paul Kerr said in his gruff voice, "I've got some good news. I'm going to be married."

"Married?" Katy didn't even know her father had dated since her mother died.

"Her name is Trish Stevenson and naturally she wants to meet you and I want you to meet Trish, so we've planned for all of us to spend the weekend together at her son's house."

Katy's work as a singer-songwriter had dried up during the years of caregiving her mother so she was free and she supposed it was her daughterly duty to go. "Where does her son live?"

"His house is northwest of Toronto somewhere. I'll call you back with the exact address. I believe it's quite rural."

"How am I going to get there, Dad? I haven't got a car."

"You can rent one. Use that credit card I gave you to buy yourself Christmas gifts." The card she'd never used because she'd felt so unloved.

When her mother was alive, her mother chose and wrapped all the special gifts. Now her father didn't have time for her. That's what that credit card stood for. "Dad—"

He interrupted her protest. "Katy, this is important to me. Please be there. I understand it's a lovely house. And Trish's son sounds like a nice fellow. You might find him useful. He's a pretty big wheel in the music business."

"What's his name?" For some reason her breath had caught in her throat. There weren't that many big wheels in the music business, but it couldn't possibly, be, could it?

Her father coughed. "His name's Adam Stevenson."

Even though she was half expecting it, she still exclaimed, "No way!"

"Does that mean no way you're coming?"

"No, no, it means that I'm astounded at what you just said. Are you engaged to marry Adam Stevenson's mother?"

"Yes. That's what I've been saying for the past five minutes. Don't you listen?"

"I am now. You're always so vague. Are you telling me that your fiancée's son is Adam Stevenson from Stevenson Music Management?"

"Yes. That's him. Have you ever met him?"

"No. But I'd like the chance to meet him."

"This is more than a chance. He's going to be your step-brother."

Katy disconnected her phone and sat on the sofa in the small apartment she shared with friends. She remembered back a few months to when she'd visited Stevenson Music Management.

Impressed and just a trifle scared she'd stood on the dense black marble floor of the large foyer. SMM was scrawled in silver across the middle of the floor and the entire area was illuminated by the natural light from the many slanted roof windows.

The receptionist with the silky blonde hair and huge blue eyes had glanced up at the line in front of her. "Next," she'd called out shrilly.

The black leather man, with the guitar case, in front of Katy, stepped up to the curved counter and mumbled something. The receptionist smiled brightly and pointed out a door that probably led into the offices.

"Next."

"My name is Katy Kerr. I'm a singer-songwriter. I want to see Adam Stevenson, please."

"In what respect?"

"I need someone to represent me."

The woman's brilliant white top teeth nibbled her bottom lip. "And you just walked in here without an appointment?"

"Can I make an appointment?"

"Not just like that, you can't." The woman clicked her fingers in the air. "Anyway, Adam Stevenson is out of town and I have no idea when he'll be back." She dragged a phone pad forward. "I can take your name and number and have his assistant call you."

Katy gave her name and number and it was written down half-heartedly. "Can't I make an appointment today?"

"His assistant is also out of the office today and she's the person to make appointments with." The woman let out a shoulder-heaving sigh. "I would advise that you phone first to see if you can get an appointment."

Katy had tried that with no result so she'd showed up in person. "What about email?"

"No emails. I am really truly sorry. Next please."

A woman with long blonde hair in skinny jeans and a denim jacket slipped in front of Katy.

As she was walking to the swing doors Katy noticed the skinny blonde was directed over to the door the leather man had gone through. She was going through that door one day, she decided as she left the building.

She slipped into the car she'd borrowed from a friend, started the engine, and prepared to back out. Great timing. A white limousine drove up and stopped right behind her. Letting out a frustrated sigh, Katy observed the man leaving the limousine through her rear-view mirror. From the back he was broad-shouldered, with thick, vital, nut-brown hair brushing the collar of his black wool overcoat. When he turned to speak to the driver opening the door, she saw his profile: Dark eyebrows over deep set eyes, a well-shaped nose and a vulnerable full mouth. His chin was strong. She wished he'd turn all the way around but as soon as the limousine door closed he walked briskly into the building and disappeared through the tinted glass doors. *Sexy*, she thought as the limo moved off. *Wow.*

She left the parking lot and swung the car onto the road. Edging slowly toward downtown Toronto from the suburban industrial estate, Katy now wondered if this morning's trip had been worth the effort. Granted, she'd actually visited the Stevenson Music Management building. Still, she hadn't come here to gawk at a music shrine. She'd thought that approaching SMM might be the first step in getting her life into order. She'd only had one gig in the past month and while she was part-owner of a vegetarian restaurant with a friend due to an inheritance from her grandparents her music career paid her bills. And she'd been doing quite well before her mother was diagnosed with cancer. Spending all her spare time caring for her mother had cut her off from the music world. Saying no so much had been a dreadful experience. At the same time as the agony of watching her mother die it was also like watching her own dreams go up in a puff of dust.

At her mother's funeral, her father, brother Robert and his wife comforted her with their presence. However, as soon as the funeral was over they all took off and left her to flounder with no support. She'd even had a boyfriend at the time. Yet he hadn't been able to spare a moment off work to pay his respects. To add to her heartache, Katy had broken up with Ken a week after the funeral. All he cared about was his next real estate deal. One day she would hear about him being taken to a hospital to have a cell phone removed from his ear.

Katy drove through the city to where she lived. The residential street was crowded as usual, but she managed to find a spot not far from the apartment she shared with her friends, Heather and Joe. As she stepped from Heather's car she slipped the keys into the pocket of her black wool jacket. She noticed the blue sky from this morning had turned gray and now icy little snowflakes pinged at her forehead and scattered over her long brunette hair. The wind lashing her best black slacks against her thighs was bitter cold. Shivering, Katy rushed past the row of narrow brick houses that were either rental apartments or had been renovated by trendy couples. The frosty weather was an indication Christmas was only a few weeks away. She'd promised to spend the season at home with her family, when, according to her father, they would also sort through her mother's belongings and decide what possessions they wanted to keep. Her father planned to sell the suburban house in January and go north to live up in Muskoka in his newly winterized lakeside cottage. When the cottage was also sold, he would settle into his retirement in a condominium near a golf course. To Katy that meant she would probably never see Paul Kerr again. He was a golf fanatic.

With stiff, cold fingers Katy poked her key into the lock of the front apartment in one of the houses. Katy had only intended to share until she married Ken. Now she wasn't marrying Ken, finding a place of her own was imperative. Darn Ken. She really had held expectations for her future with him. Nevertheless, she had learned some lessons from the experience: Think before she rushed into anything and certainly never have expectations. Expectations were the cause of all of her disappointments.

At least the apartment seemed warm and friendly inside. As Katy closed the door, she heard low voices from the kitchen and smelled freshly baked cookies. Just like home, she thought, remembering her mother again, even though it had been years since her mother had baked a cookie.

She tossed her purse down on the coffee table, took off her jacket and hung it in the closet. Heather and Joe were sitting at the kitchen table. Heather was tall and thin with very short blonde hair, always a perfect new style due to her job in a beauty salon. Joe was big and good-looking, with black hair gelled back for his daytime job in the bank. When he was at home and he turned into his weekend job of a rock guitarist, his hair tended to hang in curtains through which he peered.

They both wore jeans and black sweaters.

Heather jumped up from her chair. "How did it go, Katy?"

Katy handed the car keys to Heather. "It was actually a waste of time. I couldn't get past reception. I need an appointment. Neither Adam Stevenson nor his assistant was there, so that means I have to try phoning again. Which as you know, doesn't work."

Katy smiled for a second then let the smile fade. Heather looked upset and Katy thought her tension had a lot more to do with something else than her own plight at SMM. She glanced at Joe who was plucking the form of a stick person out of a napkin. "What's the matter, you guys?"

Heather sighed. "Sit down. Have a cookie. Do you want some tea?"

"Sure." Katy pulled out a wooden kitchen chair and sat down opposite Joe. She thought his usually twinkling dark eyes seemed as dismal as the weather.

Heather served Katy with a mug of hot, steaming tea and returned to her chair. "You know my mother went into hospital today for that knee operation. Well, I have to go home and look after her when she comes out, because she won't be very mobile. Therefore, Joe and I can't get married until later."

Katy tried to take in the implications of this news. Maybe she was giving out bad vibes to everyone and nothing would go right for her friends either. "When are you getting married then?" she asked.

"We'll postpone everything until next September. By then Mom should be fine."

Katy looked at Joe. "What do you think?"

Joe crumpled the torn napkin. "She has to do what

she has to do. I'm not losing her. But I can't afford the rent here alone."

Heather said, "Would you like to share with Joe? That's what we're thinking."

"You mean me move in here permanently with your fiancé?"

"I trust you. I've known you since university. And so has Joe."

Joe grinned. "And it's not that I don't think you're the sexiest thing on two legs, Katy, but I trust myself."

Katy smiled. "Joe. I trust you. I suppose it's a good deal. I was looking for a place for myself, but half a rent is better really."

"It'll give you a chance to work on your music," Heather said.

Joe gave her a sympathetic sigh. "You can move in your things from the storage when Heather moves some of her gear out. When you have your piano here, you'll feel better."

Katy nodded. "Okay. I need a place to live anyway."

But even though her life seemed a bit more permanent by nightfall, Katy still felt frightened. In the next door bedroom, Heather and Joe were lovers. She could hear the thump of the mattress, their heightened breathing through the thin walls, Heather's ecstasy mixed with Joe's groans of pleasure. They might have postponed their marriage, but they still had one another. And here she was desperately alone in the world. Because she was supposed to be a modern, stand-alone woman, she felt guilty for thinking this way. But she couldn't help it. She was lonely. And the loneliness manifested itself into memories of the man in the black overcoat who'd stepped from the limo outside SMM today. So tall and strong looking, he was the type of man she needed right now. She imagined his dark inscrutable eyes, how he might look at her, feel in her arms, her fingers entangled in his thick hair as he kissed her.

# Chapter Two

The moment he entered the house, Adam heard music. He followed the sound, from the entrance foyer, under the arch, into the annex. The red studio door was open, and he heard Jayne singing. She possessed a much clearer tone than her mother's husky blues voice, the voice that had been the first stepping stone to his career in the music business.

His daughter experimented with some of the sound equipment. Piercing feedback screeched at him, making Adam's nerves wince. He cleared his throat. "Jayne?" She flung him a look over her shoulder and quickly pushed some buttons until the grating sound stopped. "Dad, you're home early."

"I'm not early. I'm on time. Remember, we have company coming for the weekend. You should be getting ready." His palm clenched around his car fob in his pants pocket as he controlled his temper. Lately, anger seemed to be the only way he could express his emotions. Even a warm spring day like today didn't seem to dull the edge.

"Great weekend it's going to be," Jayne retorted. "You're so damn cranky."

"Jayne," he said firmly.

Muttering under her breath, words Adam didn't want to decipher, Jayne turned off equipment until all the lights were no longer flashing or glowing. "Better?" she asked.

"Good." He really did hate himself for being mean to her. She was such a beautiful girl, with her fresh skin and shiny, nut-brown hair. She no longer looked like a little girl. Her high cheekbones were more defined, her delicate nose less childlike, her mouth wide and outlined with the palest lipstick. Her youthful body, though slender, filled out her pencil slim blue jeans and a snug red top. While she dressed like other girls her age, she also possessed a style very much her own.

"We have to discuss my music seriously, Dad. If you ever have a moment." She spoke the last sentence sarcastically and flared her nostrils at him.

"We've discussed it, Jayne. You know my opinion. I want you to get an academic education first." He heard the stern tones in his statement, the type of voice he used when he'd reached his negotiation limit with a recording company. At this moment he'd reached his limit with everything in life. He certainly knew he wasn't ready to have his daughter in the music business, enduring all the highs and lows that implied. He wanted her safe, home, here.

She poked him in the chest with a navy blue fingernail. "It's okay for you."

"I'm not an artist or a performer. I'm a businessman."

"But you deal with performers. Without performers, people like me, who want to perform, you wouldn't have a living. Would you?"

A cluster of pain knotted in his right temple. He automatically rubbed the throbbing area. "I can't deal with this now. There isn't time."

"When is there time? That's what I want to know."

Just a year ago he would have described Jayne as a rather introverted teenager. But now in her last year of high school she seemed to have gained more poise. He supposed he would have to reserve some time for her from his busy schedule, a schedule stretching beyond him into eternity, for an argument he had no intention of losing. To make her back down for the time being, he said, "After the weekend."

She snapped her fingers and performed a little spin. "It's a deal."

He said, "It's only a deal for us to talk. Nothing more."

Her face crumpled. "Why can't you just say, go ahead? Why do you have to stall me all the time? You know, I just might go put something on the internet and see if I get any action."

The ache in his temple increased and he touched the door frame. "Let's not rush into anything. Careers do need managing."

"Then manage me."

"We'll discuss it after this weekend. We don't have the time right now."

Jayne kissed his cheek. "I do love you, Dad, but you're such a tyrant. However, now you've promised me an audience I'll have a chance to persuade you to let me study music, so I'll promise you I'll do a great job of running things this weekend. I'll go change into something more alluring." She swayed her hips on her way past him.

Adam watched Jayne leave the studio. This house, with all its amenities, had been an indulgence to a dream. It was his fault Jayne was learning to use all of the high-tech recording equipment and expanding her musical knowledge. He'd given her a full platter. What did he expect? And if he didn't help then she could very well go it alone. But he really did want her to get an education first.

Adam closed the door tightly, shutting down one aggravation to face another. Now he had a family duty ahead of him.

His mother, Trish Stevenson, had phoned him at the office the other day to tell him she was engaged to be married and hoped for a June wedding. Adam had to be honest; he was stunned at her news.

"Are you sure?"

"Positive. I haven't felt this exhilarated since the day I met your father."

"And that was a mistake."

Trish tut-tutted. "If you say that, then you and Laura were also mistakes and I'll never feel that way. I'm well over your father, Adam. Paul is a wonderful man. We met at the golf club."

"That's fine, but do you have to marry him?"

"Yes. I do. I've made up my mind about this. Now I want to ask you a favor. We need to set up a family meeting before the wedding, and I was thinking, your place."

"Can't we just go out to dinner somewhere?"

"No. Paul and I have to drive down from up north and we'll have to stay somewhere. Besides, you can't get to know people at a restaurant. There's also Laura and Jason, Jayne, and Paul's daughter. We could make it a family weekend, Adam."

He knew he should delight in the chance for a weekend off, but instead the thought scared him. Work kept him on a narrow footpath. But it was a familiar path. Knowing he was free for a few days panicked him. The fast pace got him down, but he was at a loose end without it. He was hot-wired for his work.

Nevertheless, he'd realized he didn't have any choice in the matter. "I'm free next weekend. And that's it for a couple of weeks."

His mother made a speedy decision. "Next weekend it is. I know a wonderful couple who will come in and cater the entire weekend. Will you also be free for the wedding? It's about a month away."

She gave him a date and he marked it down on a blank page. Thank goodness. He was able to say, "Yes," with certainty.

"Good. Then we'll go ahead with the wedding arrangements. And one more thing, Adam, Paul's daughter is a musician. She's had it a little rough lately, not much going on for her, so I suggested to Paul you might be able to help her in some way."

Trust his mother to burden him with some wannabe at his house for the weekend. If his mother's husband-to-be was already asking for favors what else would he ask for? His mother's savings? In all the years since his mother had divorced his father, Adam had only ever met two men who interested Trish Stevenson and he hadn't particularly liked either one of them. Because his mother had done well in real estate, he was sure they'd both been after financial security.

He had a stock answer. "We'll see. I'm not promising anything."

"All right, Adam. The main thing is we all get together."

Now still questioning what his mother had dumped on him, Adam took the stairs two at a time to the landing and strode to his bedroom. Not having much time, he stripped off his clothes. Standing under steamy hot water, lathering his muscular limbs with tangy body wash, he breathed deeply to try to calm himself down.

But his brain wouldn't stop.

Fred Doncaster, his financial man at SMM, needed sorting out in Europe with the new group Kick Start.

Two of his long-time, top-billed clients, Lilah Payne and Rory Dean, had immediate problems needing attention. Actually they were fading stars. They were in desperate need of some internet celebrity. He needed to speak to his techy guy at his office for that. Maybe some of their old legendary songs would take off again and then when they released new material their stars would shine once more.

And this proposed marriage meant Jayne wouldn't be spending the summer with his mother.

This might mean he would have to take more time off work than merely the week for the wedding.

Adam turned off the shower and dried himself briskly with a fluffy white towel. With the towel around his neck, he placed his hands flat on the marble vanity top.

He stared into the misty mirror, seeing a damp, broad-shouldered, dark-haired man with too many thoughts racing around inside his head. He lifted the towel and rubbed his hair, at the same time loosening his shoulders, trying to release some tension from his body. Then the doorbell chimed and his shoulders tensed again.

He'd have to answer it unless Jayne was available.

In all honesty, he'd needed a few days off to kick back at home before this weekend. Except he wasn't sure he knew how to relax anymore. His days of vegging out on the sofa in front of a TV screen were long gone.

Releasing a breath, he wrapped the towel around his waist. From his bedroom door he called along the corridor, "Jayne, go answer the door. Please."

Jayne didn't appear and he thought he heard her shower running. He tossed aside the towel and shrugged into his navy terry robe. It was probably only his housekeeper, Stella Smith. She never used her key if there was someone home and she'd seen him in his robe a hundred times before now. Tying the belt, and unable to help himself because he seemed to do everything at an upbeat pace these days, he ran down the stairs and rapidly crossed the tiled floor.

He pulled open the door. It was on the tip of his tongue to say, "Hi, Stella," but he bit back the words. The slender woman wearing high-heeled silver leather shoes and a black suit with a short skirt and a hip-length jacket was definitely not his housekeeper. Her clothes appeared quite businesslike, but her brilliant green eyes, high cheekbones and lots of thick shiny brown hair cascading around her shoulders made him lift a hand to his ruffled wet hair to flatten it. He saw lots of good looking people in his line of work but she was, well, he couldn't think of anything but—wow.

Her fingers with silver polished nails, clasped around the strap of a purple suede bag hanging from her shoulder. "Mr. Stevenson?"

Adam shifted his bare feet on to a rug, thinking about the people who were to arrive tonight. The caterer was someone he'd never met. So he said, "Hi. Are you the caterer?"

The woman in front of him let out a breath from between her perfect white teeth and desirable lips. "No. I'm not the caterer. I'm Katy."

Adam looked at her again. "I don't know any Katy's."

"Maybe you don't," she said sternly. "But you do now. I'm Katy Kerr. Paul Kerr's daughter. Your mother is going to marry my father."

Whoops. He hadn't given Paul Kerr's daughter a thought as to what she might be like. And wasn't she a musician? He could see this girl on stage with the lights flashing around her and the wind machine blowing her hair. No has-been or wannabe here.

"You do know that your mother is going to marry my father?"

"Yes. Sorry. I didn't mean to be rude." He stretched out his hand. "I'm Adam Stevenson."

She folded her hand into his and he felt the electricity pulse through him. *Oh, yes. Definitely, wow.* "You're early."

"I know. Sorry. I left downtown with time to spare and found the place easily. And I got you in the middle of your shower." She glanced at his wet hair.

"No. I'd finished the shower. Come on in." He ushered her into the house and closed the door. "You'll have to wait around. My housekeeper isn't even here yet and she's supposed to arrive before the caterer."

"Then you should be pleased I'm not the caterer." She glanced around the foyer. "What a cool house."

"I had it built with everything I ever wanted in a house." Adam couldn't keep his eyes off her. She was gorgeous. Absolutely.

"It's really great."

*So are you.* He directed her to the double doors that led into the spacious, high-ceilinged reception room, where French doors looked out on to the red-tiled patio and a satiny lawn. She slipped the purple bag down on his couch and patted the cushion. "Such soft cream leather."

"Then make yourself comfortable for a moment. I'll see you in a while," he said and returned upstairs.

Hanging out of her bedroom door, her hair wrapped in a towel turban, Jayne asked, "Who was that, Dad?"

He was breathing hard from the race up the stairs. "Er, Paul Kerr's daughter."

"Grandma's fiancé's daughter?"

"Right." He nodded.

Jayne gave him a funny look. "What's her name?"

"Kerr, same as her father's."

"Her first name?"

"Katy. Can you go and entertain her? Pour her a drink. She's in the front reception room."

"Is she pretty?"

Pretty was an understatement. She was beautiful. "I didn't notice. I have to get dressed. Just go and look after her."

Adam closed his bedroom door and pulled on some clean briefs. He dried his hair, shaved, and then selected ivory cotton pants and a long sleeved black silk shirt from his closet. He shrugged into the shirt and zipped his pants.

He had just put on comfortable black loafers when his phone jingled with one of his band's ring tones. He picked up the phone from his dresser, disconnected the call, and slipped the phone into his pocket. He knew it was his assistant, Alison, and that she'd probably call him back later. Right now he didn't have time for discussions. Alison didn't usually bother him with unimportant stuff so it would be important. Yet he still felt as if he was deserting his work for not wanting to answer the call.

# Chapter Three

Adam Stevenson had left the room ages ago now, but Katy still saw him. Deep-cheeked, masculine features with glittery blue eyes, a white, taut smile and a tense jaw. And very muscular legs exposed by his short robe. To sum him up she would say Adam Stevenson was handsome, desirable, and impatient.

Katy twisted on her heels to look at the room, hoping the subtle elegance would take her mind off him. Except it was his home and she saw him choosing the interesting color-splashed canvasses on the walls, the antique oak tables and cabinets, and the thick, oriental rugs resting luxuriously on the polished hardwood floors. It was difficult to believe she was actually inside Adam Stevenson's home. Her heart had pounded like a jackhammer as she'd driven through the iron gates into the driveway and up to the sprawling wood and stone house. Actually, she'd been in a state since her father had told her who he was marrying. Should she take advantage of this meeting or should she play it cool and pretend she didn't need help with her career?

Katy suddenly realized she wasn't alone in the room. A young woman had appeared at the open doors. She was extremely pretty with casually upswept brown hair and a pair of very long pink and black earrings swaying against her delicate neck. The earrings perfectly matched her black silky dress dotted with pink flowers. On her feet were pink suede sandals with high heels.

Adam's wife? She was very young for him. Her father, typically, had only given her the bare facts. Katy felt out of her depth and some of the glitter faded. "Hi. I'm Katy Kerr."

The woman come forward extending a slim hand with dark blue painted fingernails and a number of silver rings containing an assortment of inlaid symbols and different colored gems. "Pleased to meet you, Katy. I'm Jayne Stevenson, Adam's daughter."

Daughter. Then he was married. Katy shook Jayne's cool bejeweled fingers. "Hi, Jayne."

"Nice to meet you. I'm the hostess for the weekend."

"Is your mother not here?"

"No. She died when I was a kid. They weren't married. I don't remember her except I've seen pictures and videos of her. She was Rachel Frank. Do you remember her? Anyway, don't say anything to Dad that I've told you. He likes to keep it secret that I'm her kid so I don't get hassled. He never married anyone else. Not sure why. He's had lots of girlfriends. No one I liked."

Katy felt that she was probably being told too much, but she smiled and said, "I won't say anything." She recalled that Rachel Frank had died of an overdose or suicide, or whatever—Katy hadn't been very old herself at the time and had been into other singers. Although, Katy's brother was a fan she'd never heard of any affair where Rachel had a daughter, but she could understand Adam's desire to keep his daughter from any media attention that might result from having a famous mother. For some reason Katy felt relieved Adam wasn't married.

"Anyway, I'm supposed to get you a drink? Do you want anything?"

"Not really. I haven't even brought in my luggage yet." Katy could do with some fresh air. The atmosphere, her clothes, her skin, everything, seemed tight and cloying and she could feel a throbbing pressure over her eyes.

"Let's go get your luggage," Jayne said. "And I'll show you to your room. You might like to use the bathroom. Dad probably didn't think of that."

"No. He didn't." Katy was pleased to have someone here who seemed to be on her side.

Jayne beckoned for Katy to follow her to the front door, where the girl jammed open the door with a brass door cat-shaped stop. Outside, they walked over the warm asphalt to the maroon rental car that she'd parked at the rear of a black BMW and a smaller white, sporty Audi.

"Dad's is the BMW," Jayne said. "Mine's the Audi. Dad bought it for me for my birthday. I just got my license."

"Lucky you," Katy said. Was Adam another father, like her father, who gave his daughter gifts to satisfy a father's guilt trip?

Jayne stopped at the rental car. "Is this yours?"

"I rented it for the weekend." Katy opened the trunk of the Ford and lifted out a blue garment bag and a bulky overnight bag.

"Do you live far away?" Jayne asked.

Katy closed the trunk. "I'm downtown Toronto."

"I'd like that. I mean, this is a great place, but it's

Dad's dream, not mine. Know what I mean?"

"I know exactly what you mean." Katy smiled. She liked Jayne.

Jayne picked up the garment bag. "Are you married?"

"No."

"Do you have a boyfriend?"

"Not at the moment."

"I guess you would've brought him along if you had."

"I don't know about that. This is family stuff. Right?"

"Right."

Katy glanced at Jayne easily handling her suitcase. "Are you sure that bag isn't too heavy? It does have wheels."

Jayne tested the heaviness. "It's fine. I'm strong. Dad has a gym and a pool here. I swim and exercise."

"There's a pool and gym inside the house?"

Jayne grinned. "He's got everything in this house he ever wanted, including a music studio. Are you interested in music?"

*A studio. Oh, wow.* "I'm a musician."

"Really." Jayne smiled. "Oh, great. That's wonderful. I sing but I like to write songs as well. Though I need some help sometimes. Could you help me?"

"I might be able to. We'll see. I'm only here for the weekend."

"Yes. But we're going to be related so we'll see each other again. We can combine our talents. Okay?"

"Possibly," Katy said. She might have a chance to work with Rachel Frank and Adam Stevenson's daughter. Her father had dumped her inside a dream.

"And maybe," Jayne said as they walked back to the house, "we can take some videos of me singing and post them on the internet."

"We could do that," Katy told her. "But can't your father help you? He might think a career should go in another direction."

"He won't help. He doesn't want me in the business."

"Ah," Katy said. "Not ever?"

"I don't know. He uses the excuse that he wants me to get a university degree first, but I don't see why I can't do both."

"Do you think he's worried about the dark side of the business, considering what happened to your mother?"

"Definitely he is. But I'm not like her. I'm more like him." They reached the front door. "So do you think we could team up?"

"Do you play an instrument?"

"Not really. Mainly I sing. What about you?"

"I play the piano. I sing. I like writing songs the best."

"You could write me songs to sing then?"

Katy nodded, not wanting to raise Jayne's hopes too high. She didn't know how this weekend, or even her father's marriage was going to work out yet. And she really didn't want to get between a father and daughter feud.

Jayne closed the front door. "Everything's in this annex," Jayne informed her as they walked beneath an arch. "Dad's given you the bedroom next to the studio. Everyone else gets to stay upstairs."

"Who else is coming?" Katy asked, pleased to get away from the subject of Jayne's music career.

"Aunt Laura, Dad's sister, and her boyfriend Jason Riley. And then Grandma and your father."

"Have you met my father?" Katy asked.

"No. Not yet. Have you met my grandma?"

"No. I'm looking forward to meeting her."

"You'll like her. She's great. Not as mean as Dad."

"Your father's mean?"

"Not really. But he's a cranky workaholic. Aunt Laura says he'll just keel over from a heart attack one day and that will be it. He won't slow down."

"He obviously likes his work."

"Oh, yes. He does. However he uses it as a shield so he doesn't have to get close to people and worry about everyday stuff. Know what I mean?"

"Yes. I do know. My father was the same when I was growing up."

"Will he be okay with my grandma then?"

"He's retired now. He's got more time."

"I hope so. I'd like her to be happy. Anyway," Jayne tapped a red door as they passed by. "That's the studio. There's a suite in there for musicians to stay in." Jayne stopped walking and pushed open a white door. "This is your room. If you pull back the vertical blinds you will see the pool behind all those plants. There's a door in the corner you can use to reach the pool. The water is heated. If you didn't bring a swimsuit there are some packages containing new suits in the changing hut. They are plain black but not bad." Jayne reverted to the wheels and propped Katy's suitcase beside the closet. "Oh, and the gym is next door to the pool. There's a sign on the door. Also the entire house has wireless internet in case you brought a laptop with you. I can give you the code."

"I didn't bother," Katy said. "I didn't think I'd be able to get online." Although she'd bought along her phone that needed charging. She'd thrown the adapter into her luggage at the last moment. One of her bad habits was never turning on the phone or not having it charged up. She still relied on landlines, much too all her friends' despair.

"Well, next time you'll know," Jayne said. "If you want to check your email or anything, Dad has a spare computer in his office, or you can use mine."

"Thank you. But it's okay. I get my email on my phone."

"That's great then."

Jayne gave her a chance to look around and Katy really liked the room. The walls were a light green with stenciled flowers and matched the duvet cover. The white cupboards and the dresser were practical. The watery light from the pool made the light in the room waver like a tropical underwater paradise. "It's beautiful in here."

Jayne nodded. "Neat, isn't it? I sometimes sleep down here. I like to hear the sound of the water. I know it's open to the outside through the pool but you don't have to worry, the house is all hooked up to a security company and if you open the wrong door at the wrong time of day the alarm goes off and they send a guy over."

"Which translates to don't open the wrong door," a voice said.

Katy turned around. Adam, now dressed in a pair of nicely fitting slacks and a black shirt, gripped the top of the door frame with both hands. With his taut smooth jaw freshly shaved, his glittery blue eyes seemed more prevalent, and his hair was the same nut-brown as his daughter's. Now dry, it was glossy and thick.

Katy swallowed. "Thanks for this room," her voice sounded husky. "It's beautiful."

"I thought you'd like it. It's close to the amenities."

His smile was as tight as the body that strained beneath clothes. He was a man who appeared wired for action; his body all hard muscle under his well-dressed veneer.

"I see your luggage is in. Did Jayne get you a drink?"

"Katy didn't want a drink right away. She wanted her luggage and to see her room," Jayne told him. "Eh, Katy?"

"That's right. I wanted to get settled in first, before the drink."

"Great." Adam lowered his arms and shifted out of the doorway. "Have you settled yet?"

"Let her freshen up, Dad," Jayne said. "She'll meet you for the drink."

"Okay." Adam left them alone.

"Thanks," Katy said.

"He's so used to giving orders and getting all his ducks in a row that he forgets people aren't robots. Take your time, Katy. I'll see you later. I have to go see the caterers."

Katy let out a breath as the door closed. She slipped off her heels to give her feet a rest and walked into the huge bathroom. She used the toilet and washed her hands, drying them with the clean fluffy towel. She brushed her hair in her room, smoothed her jacket down over her skirt, stepped back into her shoes and wondered what would have happened if Adam had been in his office that day she'd visited SMM and she had, by some fluke, been able to meet with him. Would she have been able to stand opposite him to ask if he would represent her?

Katy closed the bedroom door and retraced her steps to the archway that led from the annex. She found

Adam in the room she'd been in before. He was standing by a cabinet with a bottle of white wine in his hand.

"Hi," she said.

He turned around. "What can I get you?"

"That white wine is fine."

He released two glasses from overhead hooks.

Katy fastened her eyes on to his back, where his shirt stretched over his firm flesh and she experienced a flash of recognition. Had it been Adam who had stepped from the limousine that day when her car had been blocked in?

Adam began to deal with opening the bottle. "You're quiet."

"I don't believe in wasting words." To relax, she stepped back a few paces and shifted her shoulders inside her suit jacket. She could actually hear her heart pounding in her ears. Had she actually been dreaming about Adam Stevenson these last few months?

He handed her a glass and raised his own glass into the air. "Cheers."

Katy lifted her glass. "Cheers."

As they moved into the center of the room carrying their glasses, Adam solved the conversation problem by asking the obvious question. "What do you think about our parents' plans to get married?"

Katy gave the obvious answer. "I haven't had much time to think. I only knew last week."

"It was such short notice I'm skeptical."

Katy hadn't really expected any opposition to the marriage plans. She had, maybe foolishly, thought the Stevenson family might be in full agreement. "Why would you be skeptical?"

"My mother's been divorced for over twenty-five

years and she's never shown the slightest inclination of wanting to get married again until now. So your father must be something."

Katy wrinkled her brow. "You haven't met him yet?"

"No. Just tell me I don't have anything to worry about; he's not after her money or her property."

Her father had faults but he certainly didn't need to marry for money. "Of course not. He retired from management in an engineering firm, with a good pension. He sold a house in the Toronto suburbs in a high-end neighborhood at the beginning of this year. He also sold a lakeside cottage and now owns a condominium. He's made some fantastic investments over the years. Actually, he's rolling in it. Possibly your mother is after his money."

Adam raised an eyebrow. "No way. She made a bundle in real estate and invested wisely. She owns a property in Muskoka."

"Well then, if money isn't their motive, then maybe they're in love. I mean, that was my first thought." She hoped she was right.

"What was your second thought?" Adam asked.

"Why would you think I had a second?"

"Because you mentioned your first thought. If it was your only thought then you'd have said only. So what was your second? We all have second thoughts."

Katy added "pedantic" to all his personality traits. "Well, it could be that I thought it was fast, as my mother only died a year ago."

"Then you're against him getting married again too soon?"

"I'm not against it. He's a grown-up. He can do what he wants." Katy had no desire to put her father into a bad light. If her dad really loved Adam's mother, she could put the relationship in jeopardy if she said anything negative about him.

"You're probably right. We haven't seen them together so we'll reserve our judgment until we do."

"You're okay if they're marrying for love then?" Katy felt a little strange to be discussing love with Adam especially if he was the man who'd firmly starred in all her latest fantasies.

"Of course. That's what marriage is all about, isn't it?"

His gaze settled on her face and Katy fought breathlessness. However, she was pleased he felt that way about love and marriage. It made him more human even if she wasn't sure she wanted him to be more human, because it made him appealing despite the obsessive personality toward work that put her off. "Yes," she said. "Love is what it's all about. I suppose."

"But you're not sure?"

"I'm not married."

"Me neither, and never have been regardless of the daughter."

"Then we have no idea, do we?"

"Probably not. However, I would've married Jayne's mother, but she didn't want me, or the baby. She told you who she was, I guess. She always does."

Katy tried to imagine him younger and in love with Rachel Frank. Now he didn't appear to be a man who could fall in love very easily. He was terribly uptight. "Yes. She did. It was tragic what happened."

"It was. But some people can't handle talent or fame. Although in Rachel's case, I don't think she could handle being human." His smile was edgy.

Katy let out a breath. The conversation was heady and heavy. "But you loved her?"

"I don't know now. I was infatuated by an image, a voice, a style. Not sure. But I was certainly in lust." His smile was wry.

Katy let out a deep breath. "Well, you have a very beautiful daughter from that—lust, so maybe ..."

He grinned. "The pleasure was worth it?"

Katy couldn't believe she was standing with a glass of wine in her hand discussing sex with Adam Stevenson. "Was it?" she asked with a small laugh, trying to lighten the subject.

"Yes. Jayne's lovely."

"She is." Katy changed the subject. "Is your father still alive?"

"Sure is. About three years after the divorce Dad married a woman from Florida. I was shunted north and south like a commuter flight until I was old enough to run my own life and the joint custody didn't matter."

Katy heard some hurt in his voice. No one ever escaped pain. Adam had experienced his share. But still, he had a great deal of everything else that surely made up for a little personal discomfort. He was a powerful man; the yes or no to a music career for a lot of desperate artists. He was fabulous looking, and he had a great daughter.

"Do you still go down to Florida?" she asked.

"If I can get away in the winter months. My father is Jayne's grandfather, after all. And I have a place there."

Of course he had a place there. Katy wished her father had told her more about the Stevenson family. If she'd come armed with information, she might not feel as if she were staggering around in a swamp. Although, she had known about him. She'd seen him that day step-ping from the limousine and she'd been infatuated with him ever since. She just hadn't known he was the same man she'd desperately wanted to meet.

Adam walked to the cabinet, poured more wine, held the bottle up to Katy. "Want some more?"

"No. I'm fine," she said.

Adam was appearing as if he was ready to speak again when Jayne came to the door.

"Dad. Everything's under control in the kitchen," his daughter said.

"Good. What time is dinner?"

"Seven. Everyone should be here by then. Laura and Jason are usually late. Not because Laura likes being late but because Jason can't get his act together most of the time."

"Jayne," her father warned.

Katy's silver polished nails dug into her palm. She sure hadn't given any consideration to the added stress an extended family would bring to her life.

A pop tune ring tone sounded in the room. Jayne swore. Adam frowned at her, put his hand deep into his pocket and pulled out a phone. He stared at the dis-played name and took the call. "Fred. How are you? No. That's not good enough. They are worth more. I don't care about any of that. Remind the promoters that the group is about to sign with a major label. Okay. Keep talking."

Adam disconnected that call and was about to shove the phone back into his pocket when it rang again. He said, "Hi, Alison. Yes, I talked to him. What else is there? Okay. Send Gary North and book me out on Monday. That's the soonest I can get there. In the meantime I suppose we'll have to cancel Tuesday's concert in Seattle. Yes. Thanks. Keep me informed. I'll be here all weekend. Have a good weekend yourself."

Adam pushed the phone back into his pocket and picked up his glass. He seemed distracted as if his mind was now filled with his new problems.

Katy heard Jayne say, "I'll go check on dinner again."

"Great idea," Adam said and his voice sounded husky and vague.

Jayne left, and through the tense silence Katy heard ticking. Her gaze traveled around the room searching for the clock. She saw the tall brick fireplace with the hearth of brilliant scarlet and black inlaid tiles. Fresh white daisies stood on the wide mantle shelf in a turquoise vase. Next to the flowers she discovered a big wooden clock with gold hands. With each shift of the hands, a loud tick was heard. She stared at the time. She had only been here for a little over an hour but it seemed to be forever.

Despite all the negatives about Adam Stevenson, Katy knew that she was really attracted to him, probably already in love, and she knew she was going to need a lot of strength to get through this weekend and maybe the rest of her life if Adam was to figure prominently in it. "I think I'd like to go to my room," she said hearing her voice sound as if it wasn't really part of her anymore.

"See you at dinner," he said.

He didn't seem to care that she was leaving so Katy put down the glass and found her way to her room. She unpacked her clothes, hung the few things she'd brought with her in the huge closet, and took a shower in the massive bathroom. She put on a short black dress with a V-neck edged with silver that matched her silver shoes. She blow-dried her hair that had got damp in the shower. She still couldn't believe that the man she'd seen that day outside SMM had been Adam and that her father was actually going to marry his mother.

She walked back to the reception room anxious about being alone with Adam once again, but when she got to the foyer, she heard voices. People were arriving for the weekend.

"Katy," her father said when he saw her and she thought he overdid his hug after a six-week absence. He'd not even hugged her that way when her mother died. He had kept himself very distant. But he seemed jovial tonight, and she admitted he did look extremely handsome in a charcoal herringbone suit and a dark blue shirt and tie. His usually fuzzier curly hair had been neatly trimmed and his round handsome face was clean-shaven. Maybe she was too uncharitable about him sometimes, but here he was, putting up another barrier between them in the form of an attractive silver-haired woman.

Draped in a blue pant suit, Trish Stevenson gave Katy a perfumed embrace. "I've been so looking forward to meeting you, Katy. It's a shame your brother and his family can't be with us this weekend. But they spoke to us on the phone last night." Trish put out her arm to include Adam. "It's good to see you as well, Adam. I think it's been months since we last had lunch." Trish spotted her granddaughter. "And Jayne, honey, how're you?"

"Fine, Grandma." Jayne hugged Trish with genuine affection.

Trish introduced Adam and Jayne to Paul. "My fiancé." She presented him proudly.

Katy watched Adam shake her father's hand, saw

the two men evaluate one another, and then her father glanced over Adam's shoulder and winked at Katy. She knew that he saw the same handsome, powerful man she saw, but he was figuring Adam for a career boost, not a man his daughter could fall madly in love with.

# Chapter Four

Adam saw his mother hold up her hand to display a cluster of shimmering diamonds for everyone to admire, and he gave Paul Kerr a discerning stare. Katy's father had slipped on a pair of gold-framed glasses to look at one of the paintings on Adam's wall and Adam had to admit that Katy was probably correct in saying her father was well-heeled. He had the attitude of a retired, astute businessman. A few weeks down the road the Kerr's would be part of the Stevenson family. One part of him felt exhilarated and the other frightened because he did find Katy extremely attractive especially in that black and silver gear.

The doorbell rang again and Adam went to answer it. It was his sister, Laura. She wore a winter-white linen suit, high heels to match, and her long golden hair flowed down her back. He glanced behind her. "No Jason?"

"No. He phoned at the last minute to say he was tied up. He'll make it here by lunch tomorrow. Therefore, I took a cab, so there wouldn't be two cars."

"Smart move." Adam placed her luggage with the other bags.

Laura pushed back her hair and shouldered her purse. "I'm amazed that you've set yourself free from the office."

"He still has phone calls," Jayne said coming into the hallway. "How are you Aunty Laura?"

Laura smiled affectionately at her niece. "I'm fine. How's it going with you?"

"Fine."

Laura eyed Adam. "Got around your dad yet?"

"I'm trying."

"He'll soften one day, don't worry. We have to distract him with a beautiful woman."

Adam saw Jayne indicate the entrance to the reception room. "He's got one in there. Katy."

Laura's brow furrowed. "Katy?"

"Paul's daughter," Adam interrupted.

"You mean she's a stunner?"

"She's attractive." Adam understated his interest.

"He's not telling the truth," Jayne remarked in a soft, slightly accusing voice. "She's extremely pretty. And nice."

His sister was smiling at him. "Are you interested Adam?"

Adam didn't know what he was at the moment. His feelings actually confused him, rare for him. "Jayne, go check the kitchen."

His daughter saluted with a glance at Laura. "Right. Sir."

When Jayne was gone his sister nudged his arm. "Come on. Introduce me to Katy. If Jayne has noticed you are interested, she must be something."

"I've only been polite." Adam insisted, but he knew he was lying. Katy turned him on. But he'd met lots of women who turned him on and they'd become immediate conquests, whether he fulfilled his mission or not. Katy was a different matter. She would be family.

Laura laughed. "It's about time you met someone and got serious. Jayne doesn't realize it but it would set her free from you."

"Laura. Don't interfere."

"She deserves at least a chance at her music career and you're mean to stop her. You'll regret it, Adam. She'll leave you for good."

Adam didn't need this. "I'll deal with it."

"I hope so before it's not too late for you. Come on. I've met Paul once before. Now I want to meet Katy."

Adam introduced Laura to Katy, served more drinks, and went to the kitchen to find Stella, his elegant, white-haired housekeeper. Jayne was organizing the caterers, whose names were Doug and Ellen Stern. As Adam watched his daughter, he found himself once again noticing that Jayne was very much her own person.

•

Katy relaxed with Adam gone.

Laura, who stood beside her, said, "How are you doing, Katy?"

She forced a bright smile for Adam's sister. "I'm doing fine."

"That's good because our family is a bit overwhelming at times. And Adam can be downright unsociable. But then he runs a big ship."

"He does," Katy agreed, but didn't want to talk about Adam. "Do you work with Adam?" Laura was a very attractive woman.

"No. I run a child care business. It's a bit like a pet-sitting service, except it's for kids." Laura smiled.

"How does it work?"

Laura touched her hair and the antique sapphire engagement ring she wore sparkled. "It's an agency called KidMinders. We send staff out to people's homes. Say to make lunch for kids if their mothers are out all day. Or someone will be there when they come home from school."

"What a marvellous idea. I always had my mother at home, but I know lots of children who didn't."

"Exactly. I came up with the idea because of Adam. When Jayne was younger and they lived closer to the city she was often alone at crucial times and I used to get called over to watch her." Laura glanced around her. "They had a really nice older home, lots of space, but of course there is more here."

"This is a fantastic home," Katy said.

Laura smiled. "It's got everything but I still think it's a little far away from the action for a teenager. But," she hesitated for a moment. "Adam is very protective of his daughter. Do you know who her mother was?"

"Yes. She told me. Jayne's lucky she has a doting father."

"That's true. But she could do with a woman's influence."

"That's up to Adam, isn't it?" Katy said.

"True," Laura mused. "But he never settles with anyone. Actually, he rarely brings a woman into the family circle."

"It doesn't seem as if he has time for anyone."

"That's true. They probably leave after the first date when he takes off for Europe or somewhere. So what do you do for a living, Katy?"

"I'm part-owner in a restaurant and work there occasionally, and when I can get the gigs I'm a singer-songwriter. I play the piano."

"A Sarah Mclachlan thing?"

"Well …" Katy shrugged her shoulders.

"You should get Adam to help you then."

"I haven't done much lately. My mother got sick and I became her caregiver. I've sort of slipped off the radar, so to speak."

"Then you need Adam's help even more. He could either be your manager to at least put you on to someone in his company."

"I don't want to bother him. This weekend is family stuff."

"Yes. But you can ask him."

Adam returned and stated that they were going to start dinner. His dining room, with more views of the red stone patio and the lawn, held a long table. A pristine lace cloth was set for seven, with glistening crystal glasses and sparkling silver. A bouquet of fresh flowers stood in the middle. Jayne had arranged the seating: Paul and Trish next to one another, Laura and Katy on the opposite side and Jayne and Adam at each end. Katy happened to be on his left.

"Paul wants to know if there are any golf courses close by he can treat you and Jason to on Sunday," Trish said to her son as they ate their way through the courses.

"Jason's club isn't far," Adam said. "He can always get us in. Sounds like a great idea, Paul."

Katy's father nodded. "Good. We'll arrange it when Jason arrives tomorrow then."

"I could probably get you tee times," Laura put in. "I'll call in the morning. Jason might be here too late."

"That's arranged then." Adam said, just as his housekeeper, Stella walked up to him to say he had a phone call.

"Ms. Payne," Stella said softly.

Adam excused himself.

For a while everyone at the table was silent until Trish remarked, "Lilah Payne must have Adam's rapt attention."

"I think Lilah's sick, Grandma," Jayne said. "They're canceling some of her performances on the west coast."

"Oh, dear, that's a shame. But I wish he wouldn't keep running off. That's the trouble with those big stars. They get so dependent on him."

Katy couldn't believe that the people she was with were casually chatting about a big name star Katy idolized. Lilah wrote beautiful songs that she sang while playing her guitar. Lilah was a pure artist in Katy's view.

"So what shall we do without your father, Jayne?"

"If we've finished the main course I think we were supposed to retire into the other room. Why don't we have our coffee served in there?"

"Marvelous idea," Trish said. "I'm getting stiff sitting here. Lovely chairs, but the high backs dig into my shoulder blades."

Paul was immediately on his feet to pull Trish's chair out from the table. Katy followed everyone into the other room. A caterer came in with a tray of coffee and set white cups and saucers out on one of the low oak tables. Katy sat on one of the cream leather armchairs surrounding the table.

The coffee had been poured and everyone had a cup when Adam returned.

"Sorry about that, gang," he said. "Are you all comfortable?"

"We're fine," his sister told him. "What's Lilah up to?"

"She has the flu." He sat down on the seat near Katy and moved to deal with his coffee. He stirred in cream. "We'll probably cancel the rest of the tour. I'll go out to Seattle on Monday and we'll make a decision."

Trish yawned graciously behind her hand. "I'm tired Adam. Why don't we all have an early night? Then we can have a good visit tomorrow when we're fresher."

"If that's what everyone wants then that's fine with me," Adam said.

It did seem that everyone was in agreement so as soon as the coffee was finished Katy let the others file out of the room and went to her own room. She closed the door and leaned against it. Her head ached and she wasn't sure if it was merely the strain of meeting new people or her attraction to Adam that caused it. Having thought of Adam for so many months and now with his presence constantly around, she felt quite dizzy with all the undulating emotions.

She needed to relax for a while, so she slipped out of her shoes and carried them into the room. She stood the shoes in a closet, which she discovered was a walk-in, almost as big as her bedroom in her apartment. The bathroom had a whirlpool tub. An assortment of bubble bath bottles stood on a shelf near the tub. Each label promised relaxation.

She began to undress just wanting to get into hot foamy water and enjoy herself.

•

Adam moved restlessly around the room. The last of his coffee sat on the table.

"Adam. You still up?"

It was Laura. In the past they'd often had post-mortems about family activities and she probably wanted one this evening. Adam only wanted to be left alone with his own thoughts. "Hi. Aren't you tired like the rest of them?"

Laura flung herself into a chair. "Still in a great mood, I see."

Adam ignored her comment and sat down. "Do you want more coffee?"

"No. Thanks." His sister gave him a narrow look. "Do you think Mom and Paul will be good for one another?"

"They seem compatible."

"They do. But thanks for having this weekend for us."

"I didn't really have much choice."

"I guess not. Anyway, I think Paul is a nice guy. Maybe a couple of years younger than Mom. I would imagine he was quite a hunk when he was younger. Apparently he played football in high school. And Katy's very nice. I think she's a little overwhelmed with us. Or maybe with you. Maybe she can sense you have a thing for her." Laura chuckled.

"I don't have a thing for her," Adam said, but he knew he did.

"Adam. You should back off SMM sometimes and look around you. You're cranky. You're anxious. You have no woman in your life and you're really being mean to Jayne in my opinion."

"Ah, don't keep going on about Jayne's musical aspirations. What can I do for her anyway? I'm not the answer to any performer's dreams. I can give them a set mileage then they have to go the extra hundred on their own."

"I think Jayne is willing to do that. She's like you. You went the extra mile. Look what you've achieved."

Adam frowned. "You've been on about this since you arrived. Has Jayne put you up to it?"

"No. But I've always backed her up. She's needed me. It's just that I see her growing up. She's almost finished high school. I was dating Jason when I was her age."

Adam was uncomfortable with Jayne dating, but it had been happening. She'd brought a few young men home, mostly wannabe musicians who might possibly have been using her to get to him and that worried him as well. He turned the focus on Laura. "And you're still dating Jason. When is he going to marry you?"

"He wants to get the company up and running successfully."

"It's already pretty successful in my mind."

Laura flicked back a lock of silky hair. "Then I guess I'd better start hinting that my biological clock is ticking and I'm not getting any younger."

"I would," Adam said. "The guy seems scared of marriage."

"Unlike you of course."

"I'm different from Jason. I'm honest upfront. I wouldn't mind being married, but I don't know who I would want to marry. I certainly don't keep anyone hanging on a string."

"Don't you have anyone ever?" his sister asked curiously.

"Occasionally," he said.

Laura shifted on the chair. "But you never introduce us to anyone?"

"I don't like parading women in front of Jayne."

"I dig the fatherly concern, but what about you?"

"I'm okay."

"Adam." Laura leaned forward, hands clasped on her lap. "You should be married. It would be better for Jayne. I'm not kidding. You wouldn't feel quite so protective of her. She's a woman, you'll soon have to let go. If you had someone else, then it'll be easier for both of you."

"Laura," Adam said sternly. "Cut it out. Don't interfere. Jayne and I will work it out."

Laura made a face. "I don't know how she can stand living with such a sex-starved old grouch."

He chuckled. "Are we going to have a kiddy name yelling match?"

"No. But it's great to see you smile. Maybe I should come by more often and poke you with a few truths. In my opinion it would be really nice if Katy did work out for you. I think she's perfect, fun and pretty."

"I'm not denying she's pretty," he said. "In fact, Jayne was right. I was kind of bowled over by her earlier."

"Then just go for it, Adam."

"I don't know. She's going to be part of our family. It might be awkward."

"I guess. There's always an excuse." Laura leaned over and reached around the base of the armchair for her shoes. She stood up, holding the winter-white leather pumps by the heels. "I'll quit bugging you now."

Adam also stood up and Laura kissed his cheek. "Goodnight, big brother."

He placed his arm around her waist and kissed her forehead. "Goodnight."

Adam shook his head as he watched his sister leave the room. She was a fine one to talk about relationships. She shouldn't be waiting around for a man who didn't seem to want her. But Laura had known Jason since she was sixteen and it had been an on and off-again relationship ever since. Adam recalled when they became engaged a year ago, his mother had been skeptical because they set no date for the wedding.

Not that marriage was one of the things the Stevenson family excelled at. He'd never married the woman who'd had his baby, mainly because she'd had no interest in marrying him even when he'd insisted. Laura was still single as well. And Trish Stevenson hadn't been involved in a married relationship since his dad walked out on her.

That day was still one of the days in his life Adam would always remember. After school he had walked into the suburban house they had lived in at the time to find his mother and his little sister in the kitchen. Laura was wailing as his mother threw objects haphazardly into two cardboard boxes. Trish's face was streaked with tears.

"Your father's gone," his mother said. "He came home for lunch to tell me. Now I'm packing the rest of his stuff."

A sinking sensation had moved all the way through him. Laura began to scream as if she knew what was going on. His mother had gathered them both into her arms and begun to sob so that they all shook. "He's left us. For good."

It hadn't actually been for good. John Stevenson had tried to return a couple of times but Trish wouldn't have him back. Adam was never sure what had transpired to cause the rift. He figured now that his father might have had an affair. It didn't take long for John to meet a woman from Florida named Susan on a March break week and marry her. Susan was quite a pleasant woman and she'd wanted to let John see Adam and Laura. So Adam and Laura got to spend a great deal of time in Florida, which is where he had met Rachel.

He left the room and walked to the pool. He needed some time alone. With all these people in the house to-night there seemed to be a constant hum. Likely all the plumbing working at once, he thought wryly as he sat down on a bench, where he could see the door to Katy's room through the tangled tropical plants. He wasn't sure why he had put Katy into that room, other than it was Jayne's favorite room and he thought someone younger would appreciate it. Although Katy wasn't as young as he'd expected.

He rested his arms on his knees and gazed down through the smooth surface of the water. He argued with Laura's notions, but she was right. His life was one-sided. For a start he needed to begin an exercise routine again—an hour in the gym each day followed by half an hour in the pool. He had too many periods in his life lately when he'd felt unwarranted anger—arriving home and being mad at Jayne. For what? For singing? He felt as if he were constantly running on a moving escalator. All he could think about were the problems at SMM, even when he was away from the office. He really did spend all his time in meetings, auditions, traveling, and a great deal of yapping on the phone. Not to mention a disintegrating relationship with a daughter growing up to be a young woman.

He raked his fingers through his hair in despair, knowing he couldn't go on this way, but he really had no idea how to stop or what would eventually stop him. To the outside world he had it all, but inside he knew he didn't.

He stood up abruptly and walked into one of the cabanas. He stripped off his clothes and slipped on swim briefs. The pool was a perfect place to dump his frustrations and beat the blues.

# Chapter Five

Katy's bath tub was now empty but she could still hear water trickling. Wearing a cotton night slip and running a brush through her hair, she walked into her bedroom and realized the watery sounds came from the pool. Through the glass she saw the moon sparkling on to the water. In the green watery light Adam swam smoothly, efficiently, and fast. His muscular body ate a length that might take her a few extra minutes to complete. He seemed to want to push his limits.

The steady splash, splash, splash of his movements bounced through the glass, and Katy watched wondering for a moment if this might be considered spying.

Eventually Adam slowed and he rolled over on to his back. Katy saw his skin gleaming gold in the misty light as he floated. When he rose from the pool, her eyes traced his physique in his brief black speedos. He was the man she'd desired for many months. Her dream lover.

For a brief second he bent his head and Katy thought she glimpsed loneliness. Then he wrapped a towel around his neck and disappeared into one of the two cabanas. After a while he came out dressed and Katy heard him walk past the outside of her room.

Katy slept much better than she thought she would and was awoken by a gentle splash in the pool and rose from bed. Through the window in the dusky morning, she saw Laura swimming. The Stevensons were a restless lot she decided as she showered and washed her hair, and wondered what they would do today. She supposed she was here to get to know Trish, as well as Jayne, Adam, and Laura. She felt she knew enough already. With the probable exception of her father and Adam's mother, who seemed to be in seventh heaven, everyone else was edgy.

It took so long to dry her hair, that by the time she was ready, it was a respectable hour to appear in front of the family. Wearing sandals, khaki cotton pants and a white silky V-neck shirt, Katy followed the aroma of coffee to the dining room, where breakfast was spread buffet-style on the sideboard. Her father and Trish were already eating.

"Good morning, Katy," Trish said. "Did you sleep well?"

She smiled. "I certainly did. I have a beautiful room near the pool."

"Doesn't the constant ripple of the water drive you nuts?"

Katy shook her head. "Not really."

"That's good. Although, I wonder why Adam put you there? This house has bedrooms galore."

"The room is fine," Katy said, moving over to the sideboard to choose a multi-grain bagel, strawberry preserves and coffee.

When the bagel was toasted Katy sat down with her father and Trish. She spread jam on the bagel thinking her father had put her into a terribly awkward position. Or was it her attraction to Adam that was causing awkwardness?

Her heart hammered as Adam walked in looking freshly showered and shaved, wearing faded jeans and a light blue sweater. He said good morning, picked up a plate and perused the food selection. He placed scrambled eggs, toast, coffee and juice on the table. Then he sat down next to Katy. "Food okay?" he asked in general.

"It's great, Adam," Paul said, holding Trish's hand on his arm.

Adam glanced around. "So where's Laura?"

"She took some coffee back to bed after a swim," his mother said.

"She can do what she wants. Jayne probably won't be up much before eleven. She always spends most of the weekend in bed."

Paul grinned. "I remember my two staying in bed half the day when they were that age."

Adam glanced at Katy. "Is that true?"

"Yes. It's true. I still sleep in on weekends."

"But not this weekend?"

She shook her head. "No. I thought I should join the family."

"And we appreciate the effort, Katy," Adam's mother said, finally disengaging her hand from Paul's arm and putting aside her napkin. "Paul and I are going for a stroll in the gardens. Adam has a lovely property here, Katy. You must explore it."

"I will," she said.

When the couple left, Katy let out her tension by immediately rising from her chair.

Adam glanced at her. "Have you had enough to eat?"

He was still working his way through a plate full of food.

She met his glittery gaze. "Yes. I think so. I'm not particularly hungry in the mornings. Especially after a big meal like the one we had last night. It was lovely, Adam."

He grinned. "It was lovely. So sit down, have another cup of coffee and then I'll show you around the house. You might be interested in the studio. My mother told me that you were a musician."

"Yes. I am, but I know where the studio is. I could see it alone."

He helped himself to more toast. "You didn't come here to spend the weekend alone."

"No. I came to be support for my father."

"He has plenty of support from my mother."

"I can see that. It seems like we don't have to worry about them."

Adam smiled lazily. "And they don't need us to entertain them. So relax, while I finish up here."

Katy gave up and pulled out her chair and sat down. Adam held out the silver coffee pot and Katy tugged her cup and saucer forward for him to fill the cup with the steaming liquid.

"No cream or sugar?"

"No. It's fine."

He had finished his toast, so he pushed his chair back. "So tell me about your music?"

"I write songs and perform them."

"Do you play any instruments?"

"Piano."

"Local gigs or have you been across the country?"

This is probably the scenario that would have played out if she'd been allowed to see Adam that day in his office. "Just local, although I did a couple of shows down in Buffalo, New York a few years ago."

"Do you have a manager?"

"I did have. Then my mother got sick, and I gradually just faded away from my own life and got immersed into hers."

"Your father didn't help?"

She grimaced. "I'll be truthful. He likes healthy people who can do everything for themselves. Besides, he was at work all day, away on a lot on business trips. He wasn't around much."

"Sounds like me."

"Well, then," Katy said, and drank some coffee. "You understand."

"That means you also think I'm the same?"

"Aren't you?"

"Yes. I've been working like a dog stuck on an escalator and I'm not quite sure what taking time away from work is all about anymore." He'd finished his meal so he stood up. "Would you like to see the studio now?"

She didn't have any choice. He was her host. "Yes. I would. Thank you."

"Come on."

Katy had been in music studios before. Once with Joe's band when they'd recorded a demo that included two of her songs. But they'd had to rush as they couldn't afford much studio time. She'd also played as a back-up musician to an artist who had recorded one of her songs. It hadn't been a hit. She had been negotiating recording a solo album when she'd had to quit. Now she had all the time in the world and decided to make the most of this chance to see a professional home studio that included all the standard instruments, a keyboard, a silver and black drum set, guitars, both acoustic and electric, a violin, and a gleaming black grand piano she immediately coveted. There was also an area that contained a bank of electronic recording equipment that she really had no knowledge of how to use. She preferred the sound that came from real instruments than electronically constructed riffs.

Adam stood behind her. "What do you think?"

Katy turned to look at him. He had his hands stuffed in the back pockets of his jeans and the action stretched the denim across his hips. "I like it," she said softly. "In fact, I actually love it. You're lucky."

"You can play the piano any time you want this weekend. There's nothing else happening in here."

"Thank you. That'd be great."

"And maybe sometime you'd perform for me?"

Her body weakened and she wondered if she was actually breathing. "You want to hear my music?"

"Yes, I would."

"You know," she said, "I've called your office on the phone and left messages. I went to your office one day and the receptionist took a message. That was way before Christmas."

"I don't recall getting any messages with your name on them."

"That receptionist probably just threw the slip in the waste bin under her desk. She was quite something."

He smiled. "That's Merrilee. She's the daughter of a musician. She wants to be an actress. She's very dramatic."

Katy clicked her fingers in the air and flicked back her hair, widening her eyes. "You can't believe that you can come here and see Adam Stevenson, just like that?"

Adam laughed. "She really said that?"

"Not quite, but that's how it translated."

"Okay. I see that we were meant to cross paths one way or the other. Quite a coincidence that our parents are getting married."

She glanced at the piano. "I'd like to play that piano."

"Go ahead, have fun. I have a few phone calls to make. Just make yourself comfortable in here."

When Adam was gone, Katy went over to the piano. She touched the smooth shiny cover with her fingertips and lifted it. She ran practiced fingers over the scale of C and found the instrument perfectly tuned. Compared to her piano, which needed tuning, this was a finely strung instrument.

She sat down on the stool, positioned herself and tentatively began to play a love song she had written a long time ago and had sung a few times on stage. She'd always had a good reaction from the song and she wondered if sometimes she hadn't been aggressive enough in the business. She hadn't always grabbed her opportunities. Although when her mother was sick she'd been so worn out that when she did play the piano it was merely for therapy.

She found her fingers becoming more certain on the keys and realized that she hadn't played the piano for months. Her music had always been her way of gathering peace of mind, but she had let life get her down and the music hadn't been there.

She began to play another song she had written when her mother had first been ill. She felt tears blind her as she played but she didn't care. She'd never cried over her mother's death. Now alone in a sound-proofed room she had the chance.

# Chapter Six

Adam went down to his office. He pulled the big leather chair up to his desk and sat down. He really was attracted to Katy. And he'd genuinely like to do something with her career. She was attractive, and what he'd heard of her piano playing just before he closed the door sounded good. He wondered what had happened to the messages she'd left him. He was about to punch out numbers to ask Alison, when Jayne came to the door in white shorts and T-shirt, her hair knotted upon her head.

"Dad? Are you working?"

He put down the phone. "Just a phone call."

"This is supposed to be a family weekend."

"Okay, but life doesn't stop outside this house. Did you eat breakfast?"

She raised an eyebrow. "I had an orange and a poached egg with Laura. Where were you?"

"I ate on time," Adam said pointedly. "With your grandmother."

She made a face. "I suppose I should've got up early."

"I suppose it might have been a good idea."

Jayne tucked herself into a deep leather chair and

perched bare feet on the corner of his desk.

Adam threaded his fingers together and placed them behind his neck. "So what do you think of your new grandpop?"

"He won't be my real grandpop. But he's okay. I don't think he's after her money or anything. Do you?"

"No. I thought he was a very pleasant man. So what do we do? Give our blessing to the marriage?"

Jayne fiddled with the knot in her hair. "I don't think that was ever the question. Grandma's got everything arranged. She asked me to be a bridesmaid."

"Will you like that?"

"Sure. It means a new dress."

Adam grinned. "What an avaricious attitude."

"No more than Katy. She's got what she wants now, hasn't she?"

Adam's eyes narrowed. "What do you mean by that?"

"You'll help her with her music, won't you? I know she's a musician."

"Yeah, well, she's in the studio now."

"We're going to do something together."

"You are, are you?"

"Look, Dad. I've decided. I graduate high school this year and then I'm going to take a gap. They take those in Europe. And I'll work on my music."

"What about university?"

"I'll apply during my year off."

"I don't mind the year off but I would really prefer it if you use it to study some academic courses. You can do that online."

"I don't understand. You'll help Katy, but you won't help me, your own daughter."

Adam saw tears well in her beautiful eyes. He spoke gently. "For your information I haven't helped Katy yet. I haven't heard her music. And I do think I said we would discuss this when the weekend was over."

"And I know what you'll say. It'll be, 'No, Jayne, I don't want you going down the drain like your mother did. It's too hard a business. You deserve a better life.' That's not it, Dad. I want to be a singer. Period. There's nothing else I want to be. And if I don't get out there now, I might as well forget it." She sniffed the tears away.

"There are other jobs. You can come into management at SMM."

She shook her head. "Not."

"I can't argue about this now, sweetie."

"Why do you argue at all?"

He cleared his throat. "I don't want you to be disappointed if it doesn't work out."

"Let me discover that myself."

"After university."

"Then I'll study music?"

That just might be the card he should play. "I don't see why not."

Jayne swung her feet to the floor and stood up. "I'm going to stop there because that's one of the subjects I'm going to choose. To hell with you."

She left with her head in the air and Adam sighed deeply. His only choice might be to release her to the world, the reality, and hope to hell she survived.

Feeling as if someone had scrambled his brain like the eggs this morning, Adam got up and glanced out of the front window. A champagne Lexus, Jason's car, stood outside in the driveway. He supposed he was due to be with the family again. Except it wasn't quite lunch time.

He left his study and walked along to the studio. The door was still closed. He opened it carefully. Katy was gone.

•

Katy enjoyed her morning playing the piano, but she knew she would soon have to go for lunch. She went back to her room, changed her blouse for a cooler, sleeveless one, and then went along to the reception room, where pre-lunch drinks were being served by Jayne.

Jayne handed her the requested glass of club soda filled with ice and lemon.

Laura came over with her fiancé. "Meet my man, Katy," she said and introduced him.

Jason Riley was dark-haired and good-looking in a broody way, with a whipcord lean body under his beige slacks and shirt. That Laura was upset with Jason for his not showing up last night, might have something to do with the thick atmosphere between the couple. Katy had expected this weekend to be tense, but she'd thought the causes of that tension would be her father and Trish Stevenson. As it happened, her father and Trish were having a relaxing time, seemingly oblivious to all the other family issues.

At lunch, Katy found herself beside Adam again, but this time Jason and Laura were across from her and Jayne was beside her. She wished the weekend was over sooner than it would be. A tally of the time left made the event seem like a marathon. There was the rest of this afternoon, this evening and all day Sunday. As far as she knew everyone was planning on going home on Monday morning.

"My friend Molly Dean is coming to stay for the rest of the weekend," Jayne said.

"Are you talking to me?" Katy asked.

Jayne chuckled. "Yes. I am. The men are being boring discussing politics and their darned golf game tomorrow. Don't you think?"

Katy smiled. "Absolutely. Is Molly Dean, the singer?"

"Yes. She's Rory Dean's daughter."

"That's exciting for you."

Jayne put her fork on to her empty lasagna dish. "We've grown up together like sisters, except she's not around so much anymore. She's been spending a lot of time in the studio rehearsing and recording. And she's planning a tour."

"She must be thrilled to have her career take off so quickly. I saw her on an award show not long ago. She's very good." At times during the weekend, Katy felt as if she were in the middle of a dream. It was one of those times right now.

But it was no dream. When she looked up, Adam was still there and she was still attracted to him. He was still the man when it came to music careers.

Katy's limbs felt stiff when she arose from her dining chair. There was much too much tension inside her body, she decided. As everyone was standing around trying to make a decision what to do next, she escaped to her room for a moment. Her skin felt flushed and hot and her vision wasn't exactly in focus. She knew it might be a migraine headache aura and took a couple of aspirins to try and ward off any such affliction coming on over the weekend. Since her mother's death, she'd suffered from some hideous migraines and the doctor had told her to relax.

Relax? How could she relax when she'd met the man of her dreams?

Then she added, the man of her dreams who wasn't for her. Even if he did help her with her music career, she could never see herself hooking up with Adam Stevenson on a personal level. First, he wouldn't want her. She was sure she wasn't near sophisticated enough for his tastes. And then also, she was tired of men who worked to the exclusion of a personal life.

She looked at the swimming pool and decided she needed a long, cool swim. Jayne had mentioned there were bathing suits in the swim hut, and she took one that looked her size back to her room. She quickly changed into the plain black suit and went into the water. She didn't swim too hard, always remembering her mother's warning about not swimming after meals, but she managed to cool off, and her niggling headache went away.

She picked up a towel, and as she dried herself, she pushed open the door to the gym to have a peek. She didn't expect to see Adam there, his muscles glistening and bulging under the weights he was lifting.

He saw her and said, "Hey there."

Katy tucked her towel around her neck and watched him.

Adam lowered the heavy weights on to a rack. "Keeping in shape," he said.

"You can't relax, can you?"

"No. I want to but I don't really know how."

"Swimming helps."

"Oh, I know. I've got a house full of everything any one could ever want. Do you want a turn with the weights?"

"No. It's okay. I'll go change." She couldn't stay in Adam's presence too long. He was one of those dynamically good-looking men women rarely met in real life. The type of man most women should forget about and keep as a dream lover.

•

Katy changed into shorts and joined the others on the patio. She accepted an orange drink from Jason and sat down in a chair in the shade. It seemed ages before Adam eventually appeared, wearing a pair of denim shorts and a loose golf shirt.

"Where have you been, Dad?" Jayne asked.

"I had some calls to make."

"Well, we're having a nice rest," his mother told him. "Something I think you should have. You can't seem to sit still for a moment, Adam. You're up and down like that pogo stick you used to have when you were a kid."

Trying to imagine Adam as a boy on a pogo stick, Katy watched him smile at his mother.

"SMM doesn't stop just because I have company."

"SMM never stops," Jayne said. "You don't have to take the phone calls."

Adam pushed his hands deep into his shorts pockets. "I don't take all the phone calls. Only those from the people close to me. Anyway, I wasn't only working. I took some time in the gym and went for a swim."

"That's good for you," Trish said. "Now come and sit down. Jason, please give him a drink. We'll force him to stay put."

Adam sat down on the lounger close to Katy's chair. He gave her a rather intense look and she returned his smile. At moments like that it was almost as if there was something brewing between them. But they weren't alone. There were conversations to join in with, plans to be made about the wedding. By the time the afternoon came to an end, Katy once more had a slight headache that really didn't bode well for the evening ahead. Hadn't Jayne said Molly was coming tonight?

Katy had brought with her two dresses. She had worn the short black one last night. Tonight she chose another black one, long and clingy, straight cut to her ankles, with narrow shoulder straps. She added a pair of antique silver earrings that had belonged to her mother and wore her silver shoes. She left her hair loose.

As she walked to the reception room she didn't feel ready to face Adam again and she was quite pleased to find Jason alone.

"Hi, Katy," he said with a white smile emphasized by his black shirt and white tie.

"Hi, Jason. Are we the first ones here?"

"Seems that way. I'll get the drinks. What do you want?"

"I think I'll stick to ginger ale," she told him.

"Sure thing."

He poured her a ginger ale and a beer for himself. "Cheers," he said lifting his glass. "So what do you do, Katy?"

"I'm a musician."

"Another musician? Have I heard you?"

"Not on record, maybe if you've been to some of the seedier clubs in Toronto."

He laughed. "In that case I could've seen you."

Katy smiled uneasily unsure whether he was joking or telling the truth. "What about you?" she asked. "What do you do?"

"Riley Engineering. We design auto parts for race

cars. I've dragged my brothers into it. So now it's become a family enterprise."

"Sounds interesting. It must take up a lot of your time."

"All my time," he said. "We have recently won a contract with a big racing team."

"Wonderful." Katy felt ill at ease with Jason, probably because she didn't know him very well, or maybe it was because he oozed sexuality. She could understand Laura's obsession with him.

She was pleased when the others walked into the room and helped along the conversation.

"Drinks everyone?" Adam suggested. Katy thought he looked extra handsome this evening in a midnight blue silk shirt and black trousers. He also oozed sexuality but in a different, more electric way than Jason.

"We're taken care of," Jason told him. "I was just having a chat with Katy."

"He actually had a chat with you, Katy. Lucky you," said Laura. "I'll have some wine, Adam."

Adam poured her a glass and handed it to her.

Katy watched Laura lift her glass to Jason and say, "What did you chat about?"

Jason's mouth thinned. "Small talk, Laura. Cut it out."

"If I didn't need to drink this I'd like to chuck it in your face, Jason Riley."

For a second it appeared as if there might be war but Laura seemed to draw in a deep breath and capitulate. "Okay. I'll be the model fiancée for the rest of the weekend."

As promised, after dinner, a limousine drove up to the front door of the house carrying Molly Dean. Molly was vibrant and vivacious with a deep, husky voice that wasn't at all in keeping with her appearance. She was small, dressed in a sheer, black lace top, gold leather leggings, and high heeled black shoes. Her black hair was cropped boyish.

Katy watched as she hugged Adam like a little girl and said, "Uncle Adam. I haven't seen you for ages."

"Molly." Adam gave her an indulgent grin. "How's it going?"

"Super. Like, *Pink Shoes* is going up the charts. It's exciting but Dad says I have to stay grounded."

"That's smart advice. Your dad's been there, done that."

"I know." Molly turned to Trish. "I can't believe Grandma Trish is getting married."

"Neither can Grandma Trish," Adam's mother told her in a dry tone.

Katy laughed. She didn't think that Trish quite approved of Molly. And she was right.

"She's quite a little piece," Trish commented when Jayne and Molly had left them. "She gets cheekier every time I meet her and she was such a sweet little baby girl."

Adam raised an eyebrow. "She's fine. Rory and Carolyn have brought her up well."

"I hope so. She's into something big now."

"She's young for so much fame," Katy's father commented.

"She's almost eighteen going on fifty," Adam told him. "I think she'll make out okay."

Even though he sounded quite positive, Katy noticed Adam's expression was anxious. Did he worry about Molly's sudden rise to fame at such a young age?

So many performers had hit peaks and crashed. This worry on Adam's part made Katy see Adam differently.

Not only was he a sexy man and a businessman, but he was a man who cared, a father of a teenager himself. Everything about him added to Adam's complexity and doubled his attractiveness.

# Chapter Seven

"Adam," Jason said, as if heartily bored with all the conversation about Molly Dean. "Paul and I were discussing the dart board in your family room. Why don't we all go play a few games?"

"Fun." Trish tucked her arm into Paul's. "I want to beat this man of mine at something. It's not golf yet so it might be darts."

Katy saw Adam agree that darts would be fine and they all filed to the family room on the other side of the house. Lots of comfortable chairs on a hardwood floor were set around a rugged stone fireplace and a huge entertainment center that included a large flat screen TV. Hung on the paneled walls were different family achievement certificates. There were also three very professional photographs of Jayne.

"My father took those," Adam said, over Katy's shoulder.

"Your father is a photographer?"

"He has his own studio in Fort Myers, Florida."

"He's very good. He's captured Jayne well."

"Her sweet mood," Adam remarked with a smile.

"Isn't she always sweet?"

"She's also very determined and quite stubborn."

Katy laughed. "Does she inherit those traits from you?"

"Probably," he said, raising an eyebrow.

He had moved in close to her. She could feel the heat from his body. Katy stared at the photographs trying to concentrate.

"Are you two joining us?" Jason asked.

"Sure." Adam put down his glass and touched Katy's waist lightly to move her forward.

Katy found herself on Adam's dart team. She was pleased she was quite good at the game due to her father always keeping a dartboard in their basement recreation room, the passion a legacy of his British heritage. When she threw her first dart and scored a double twenty everyone cheered.

"I taught her that," Paul said proudly. "Pleased to see you're still in practice."

"I'm not. It just came back to me." It made her remember when her father was more a part of her life, teaching her many skills, and she experienced a rare sensation of being part of a family.

When the games were over and everyone retired for the night, Katy stayed behind. She sat down in one of the big armchairs, kicked off her shoes, and tucked her legs beneath her. It was a position that likely wouldn't do her nice dress much good, but she needed some solace before she went along to bed. She rested her head on the back of the chair and closed her eyes.

"Do you want the TV on?" Adam asked.

Katy opened her eyes. "I thought I was alone down here?"

"You were. Now I'm here with you." He lowered

himself into the chair beside her. "Do you want to watch TV?"

"Not particularly."

"Did you enjoy yourself this evening?"

"Yes," she said honestly. "How about you?"

"It was fun. I forget how great it is to have the family together."

"I felt the same way."

"Did you have a good family life?"

Katy shaped her dress over her thigh with her palm. "Oh, we did when I was younger, but when my dad became a manager of his department, he worked long hours and traveled a lot. My mother was rather a loner. When her parents died and there were no grandparents left, she became even more introverted. She was ill a lot. I already told you that my father doesn't have much patience with illness."

"Luckily my mother is healthy."

"He's different with your mother. He's much more concerned about her."

Adam ran his hands back and forth on the arms of the chair. "Your father definitely seems to be a better match for my mother than my dad."

Katy thought he sounded bitter. "Did you miss him?"

"I saw him enough."

He moved restlessly and her glance went to his long muscular legs encased in the black pants. Against the midnight blue silk shirt his eyes glowed darkly. Katy had the feeling she'd better leave otherwise she might get herself into something she would regret later. She untangled her legs and stood up. She was only on her feet for a moment before Adam had joined her.

Being this close to him was suddenly like being

tossed on to a blazing fire. Adam lifted his hand to the back of her head beneath her fall of hair and urged her closer until their lips brushed. She trembled from his touch and Katy saw Adam's eyes turn very dark as he slanted his mouth over hers. Their kiss was deeply passionate and Katy felt the vibrations of his need flow through her.

When the kiss ended his mouth lingered on her shoulder. "You are so beautiful."

She rested her cheek next to his and stroked his lush hair, while his fingers slid down her thigh over her clingy dress. Her dream lover was kissing her and the feeling was exactly as she had imagined all those months ago. Her entire body was on fire.

She kissed him again and this time when he opened her mouth with his, their tongues met and she felt such a stirring inside her that really nothing else mattered more than being in Adam's arms.

He removed one earring, slipped it into the dish on the table and nibbled her ear. He did the same with the other earring. Katy knew what was coming and if she went any further with him then she wouldn't be able to face the family tomorrow. She'd be a one night stand, she knew that. By Monday he'd be back at work—didn't he mention something about a flight to Seattle? But not only that—their parents were getting married they would see one another at family gatherings. And then there was her music. If he helped her with that people would believe she'd succeeded because she'd slept with him.

"I think I should go to bed now."

Adam ran his fingers through his thick hair. "Okay, but I want you to know that I meant that kiss. I like you."

Her heart soared at his words. "I like you as well, but it's not a good idea to rush into anything."

"You're right. Come on, I'll walk you to your room."

He kissed her outside her door. When she went to speak, he placed his fingers on her lips.

"Don't say a word. A kiss is just a kiss."

Which meant to Katy it was an experience that might not be repeated and she felt the first twinge of regret.

Katy went into the room. She didn't turn on any lights. She merely stripped off her clothes and stood under a light shower for a moment. She slipped into her night slip then lay in bed, her heart pounding in her chest, her senses wound into knots. Adam Stevenson had kissed her and told her he liked her.

•

Katy was up early and so was everyone else it seemed. Her father and Trish were swimming. Laura was in the dining room drinking coffee. And Jason was outside checking out his golf clubs for the game today. She decided to go for a walk before breakfast. She didn't particularly want to see Adam anyway. She still felt his kisses upon her mouth and the passion in his arms that almost led past just a kiss.

She took to the pathways through the grounds, enjoying the green fullness of the spring garden. When she returned to the house she went into the dining room to find the entire family eating breakfast. She selected a boiled egg and toast and sat down in the chair near Adam.

"Good morning," she said to everyone in general and particularly to Adam.

He didn't smile but he gave her a very intense look.

"We're not staying over until Monday, Adam," Laura said.

"I think we'll also leave this evening," Trish added. "We have to drive back up north."

Katy couldn't go back to the apartment. Joe and Heather expected her to be away another night. "I might have to stay on," she said.

Adam looked at her. "That's fine."

"Thank you. I'll leave first thing on Monday morning."

"No rush. Even though I'll leave early with Jayne, Stella will be here."

After breakfast, the men went for their planned round of golf at Jason's golf club and Molly and Jayne disappeared.

"Don't you love men," Laura said as Katy settled with Laura and Trish on the patio chairs outside the pool. "One chance for Jason to spend time with me, one chance for Adam to spend time with his daughter, one chance maybe Katy, for you to be with your father, and they go and play golf."

Used to that sort of preoccupation from the men in her life, Katy shrugged and told the women her father had taught her to play golf.

"Then you should have gone with them, dear," Trish said. "I didn't want to play with the men, but you could have spoken up?"

"Today I'd rather stay here." And that was the truth. Katy was quite pleased to have a break from Adam for a few hours.

"I'm rather enjoying this," Trish said. "It's going to be very nice having an extra daughter."

"I'll have to get used to having a mother again," Katy

said.

Trish smiled. "I hope you will accept me that way."

"She won't have much choice, will you, Katy?" Laura said. "How long has your mother been gone?"

"A year."

"Mom knew your father before, didn't you, mother?"

*Trish looks a little flustered*, Katy thought.

"It was long before he was married to Julia."

"You knew my mother?" Katy asked, wondering if she'd been connected to Adam Stevenson all of her life? "I didn't know her, Katy. But I ran into your father in Toronto. When I was in first year university we met at a party. I thought he was a really good looking man but I never made much of an impression on him. I didn't go on to complete my degree. I met John and married him right away."

Laura turned in her chair. "So tell her how you did meet him again, Mom."

Trish raised a well-shaped eyebrow. "After Christmas I went to a golf club social with a friend in Orillia and I met Paul again. He remembered me. The next day he came to visit me, and the next, and the next. This spring he asked me to play golf with him. And the rest is history."

Katy realized she felt relief that there had been no two-timing going on over the years. But their previous connection somehow gave their present connection more believability. "It's very romantic," she said truthfully. "And you'll be pleased you play golf. That's all he wants to do with his life now that he's retired."

Trish laughed. "I've already discovered that."

Laura made a face. "Does this mean I should learn to play golf so that I can go with Jason?"

"It's not a bad idea, Laura," her mother said. "I think one of the big mistakes I made with your father was letting him go and do his own thing without my support."

"But I'm not athletic."

"You don't really have to be particularly athletic for golf," Katy said. "I manage to keep up."

"I'm not sure if hitting a ball into a bunch of holes is my game. Mother's quite good, but then she's been playing for quite a few years."

Katy smiled. She was sure her father was overjoyed he'd found himself a lovely woman who was also a golf partner. At least she hoped he was.

Molly and Jayne joined them after using the pool. They were both wearing brief bikinis. Jayne sprawled on a towel and applied sun block. When she was finished she tossed the tube to Molly, who caught it and rubbed it on her legs.

Katy knew she would never look at a Molly Dean video the same way again. In fact, she might never see any celebrity the same way again. Away from the glamour, they were very ordinary people, just extremely talented. Or maybe it was the opportunity to have been born into a family in the business.

The men returned about lunch time comparing golf scores. After a swim, they joined the women for lunch which was assorted sandwiches and salads served on the patio. The afternoon was spent lazing around talking about nothing much in particular.

•

Even though everyone's plans were to leave that evening, they didn't go until quite late. Katy had a splitting headache to match her exhaustion by the time she undressed and slipped into bed. The headache made it difficult to sleep. She tangled the duvet and twisted the pillow until she wanted to scream. All she could think of was Adam, the fact that she'd been dreaming of him for so many months and now he'd kissed her and made himself no longer a fantasy but a real flesh and blood man.

When she at last slept, she stood in the middle of a densely smoky nightclub with flashing lights and loud guitars. Drums pounded and pounded and pounded. Katy grasped the pillow and burrowed her aching head into it. Her stomach rose in her throat. She swallowed hard.

Awake now. Aware of what was happening—a migraine—she kept swallowing back nausea, while pain throbbed in her temples. Had she brought migraine medication with her? Before that she might even have to rush into the bathroom and throw up.

She did just that. She felt better, but she struggled back into the bedroom with the pain flashing in her right temple. Sitting on the side of the bed, she rummaged through her bag for the right combination of remedies that would get her through this ordeal. Why here? The last thing she needed was for Adam to see her sick. She crawled back into bed and snuggled up with the tortured pillow.

# Chapter Eight

"When will you be back, Dad?"

"Wednesday or Thursday." Adam didn't add that he would be leaving for Europe on Friday.

Jayne tossed her napkin on to her plate and slipped from the stool at the counter in the breakfast area. "Can't someone else go to Lilah this week?"

"If it wasn't Lilah maybe someone else could. But Lilah and I go back a long way. You know that." Adam finished his coffee and set the cup down in the saucer. "I'm sorry, sweetie." How often did he say that? Too many times.

Jayne looked resigned. "I suppose it's your job. I'd better go get ready. Will you drop me off at Donna's? We're going in her car today."

"Sure. I will."

When Jayne had left him, Adam finished his breakfast and went along to say goodbye to Katy. He tapped lightly on the door and upon hearing a muffled answer, he entered the room. All he saw beneath the duvet was a mass of hair. "Katy," he said softly.

When she lifted her head and he saw her pale, drawn face and darkly shadowed eyes, fear rose up through his chest. Another woman, with tumbled dark hair and distraught features crawled across the bed begging—and he almost turned away because he couldn't re-live any of the pain associated with Rachel. He knew that his relationships since Rachel had all ended by the fear that he would love too hard once again.

"I have a migraine," Katy murmured. "I'm sorry."

Adam's heartbeat returned to normal. A migraine wasn't pleasant, but it wasn't self-induced. This was Katy, not Rachel.

Adam cleared his throat. "No need to be sorry. It's not your fault. Do you need to stay in bed for the day?"

She seemed to be having a difficult time focusing her eyes on him. "Probably. But I might be okay later."

"Don't worry about leaving. Stella will be here all day. Jayne will be home later this afternoon." He realized he didn't want to go away. He wanted to stay here and take care of her. Because he couldn't stay, all he could ask was if she needed anything.

"Some ginger ale would be nice."

"We've got plenty of that. I'll deal with it."

Adam found Stella in the kitchen stacking dishes into the dishwasher. "Stella, Katy Kerr has a migraine headache. Make sure she keeps in bed all day. She can stay as long as she likes, until she's fully recovered." He opened the refrigerator and took out a couple of cans of pop. He extracted a glass from a cupboard. "Will you check on her occasionally? She might need a light meal later on when she feels better."

"Of course, Adam. I'm a migraine sufferer myself. I know what she's going through."

Adam returned to Katy's room. He placed the cans and the glass down on the bedside table. Then he sat down on the side of the bed, opened one of the cans and poured the contents into the glass. "Can you sit up?"

"Very carefully," she said wryly.

Adam rested his arm behind her. Her body felt warm and supple beneath her silky slip. Her hair brushed his jaw as he helped her drink some of the fizzy liquid. He longed to kiss her again.

She gulped down a couple of sips. "That's good."

He put the glass back on to the table. "No way are you going anywhere today. Stay another night."

"I have to return the car."

"Stella can handle that. Do you have the paperwork for the car rental? We'll just extend the lease for a few days."

He felt her body tense.

"It's on my dad's credit card."

"I'll put the extension on mine then. Don't worry about it, Katy. Don't worry about anything. Now. Where's the car paperwork?"

"It's on the dresser in the rental folder. But I can't let you do that, Adam. I'll pay you back."

Adam picked up the folder. "Forget about the car. I'll deal with it. All you have to do is sleep and get better."

She sank against the pillows. "Thank you. I'm just so used to looking after myself."

"And I'm used to looking after people all the time." He smiled wryly, thinking how much the truth that was. He had looked after his mother and Laura when his father left them. Then it was Rachel. Then Jayne. Now all of his performers. There was no problem adding another person to his list, especially Katy.

He returned to the bed and sank to the side. He stroked her hair away from her face and leaned down to kiss her gently on her cheek. "Thank you for coming this weekend, Katy."

She tentatively touched his shoulder. "Have a good trip."

As he shut the door quietly behind him, he was suddenly filled with emotion. He leaned against the wall. What was this now? He knew he'd never married after being hurt by Rachel because he didn't want to be in love. Love, he'd discovered was way too hard on him. On the other hand, what he was beginning to feel for Katy seemed more than mere lust, more like love.

He returned to the kitchen, handed the rental car papers to Stella, and asked her to extend the lease until Saturday on the household credit card.

Stella took the papers. "I will, Adam. How is she?"

"She drank a little ginger ale. But she needs to sleep. If she doesn't improve call Jayne's doctor. And I'll be checking in, Stel."

Stella patted his arm. "It's fine. I'll look after her."

Jayne arrived in her private school uniform of a blue plaid skirt, white shirt and a navy blazer with a backpack over her shoulder. Adam thought that he wouldn't see her in that uniform much longer and he felt sad. His sister was right. His little girl was all grown up.

"Where's Katy?" Jayne asked.

"Katy has a migraine," Adam told her.

"So what does that mean exactly?"

"She's going to stay here another day, probably the night."

"Okay, that's fine. She's nice. And you like her, don't you?"

Stella turned away, picked up a cloth and began to vigorously wipe a counter.

Adam let out a breath but didn't answer his daughter. He went to fetch his travel bag and leather jacket.

Jayne was leaning against his car. He opened the trunk and put his things inside. When he closed the trunk, he looked at his daughter. "Why are you staring at me like that?"

"I don't know, Dad. You don't have time for me, but you have time to worry about Katy."

"She's a guest and she's going to be a family member," he said sternly. "Remember that."

Jayne pushed her hair from her eyes. "I can't forget, can I?"

"Stella will take care of her. I won't be here much. I'm going to Germany on Friday to sort Fred out."

Jayne raised her eyes to the blue morning sky. "There isn't a chance for anyone in your life, Dad. I don't know why you even had me. Except I was a mistake, wasn't I?"

"Ah, Jayne. I love you, baby. Okay?"

"As long as it's just me."

"It's just you." They used to make a game of that. Over the past few years it hadn't really been necessary to play the game. He'd been extra discreet with the few women he met. But they hadn't been important anyway. Katy, he knew, if he let her, could become important.

Adam opened the car doors and walked around to the driver's side.

Jayne slipped in beside him, slammed the door and fastened her seatbelt. "Dad. Don't make a fool of yourself." She tossed her backpack on the rear seat.

He started the engine. "What are you talking about?"

"You know. I saw you look at her all weekend."

"I thought we'd finished that discussion."

"I just want to add this: Anything you do could be

embarrassing. For me, Grandma, and for Katy's father."

He patted her knee. "I certainly wouldn't embarrass anyone." And he was pretty sure that would be true. He didn't have time for a relationship with Katy.

•

Adam parked his car in the back parking lot of SMM and slid his security card through the machine by the door. He walked the long corridor to his big corner office that was decorated in the Stevenson Music colors, silver and black.

Alison, wearing a black pant suit, with her dark hair pulled back from her face, was sitting at her computer in her front office appearing frazzled, as if she hadn't slept all weekend. Adam didn't ask. If Alison let go she wouldn't stop telling him all of her hassles with her husband, Tom Fortune, who was also an SMM employee. Tom was away so much he had barely seen his five-year-old son grow up.

However, he did need to know something. "Have you ever had any messages from a musician named Katy Kerr?"

"Messages?"

"Phone messages. Probably from reception out front."

"Merrilee Merrilee," Alison said, making a face. "I don't know why you keep her."

"She's okay. Did you get any messages passed on to you for me, probably from back before Christmas?"

Alison gave him a look. "It's pretty well summer now."

"I know, but these messages were never answered and I want to know what happened to them."

"I don't recall any Katy Kerr name. Unless I put them

on Rod Deerman's desk for him to contact."

Everything they felt wasn't important went to Rod who usually was able to tell the person they weren't talented enough for SMM representation without causing too much disappointment.

Adam walked into Rod's office. The desk was littered with papers. He'd been away for months dealing with various issues around North America. Adam found a stack of phone messages on a spike. He pulled them off and went through them. Sure enough, two from Katy. Merrilee had drawn smiley faces on each one of the slips.

"Got them," he told Alison and went through to his office and sat down at his long oak desk. He put the two messages between the pages of his daytimer but not before recording the number in his phone.

Alison came in and handed him some papers. "Here's your boarding pass. Make sure you have your passport. It's only Seattle but travel to the US requires a passport now. You'll arrive late so I've booked a limo for you to take you to the hotel. And call Fred. He's having mega-problems. I've booked a flight to Munich for Friday evening. Are you okay?"

"Why shouldn't I be?"

"I don't know. You look a bit dazed."

"I actually had some downtime. I don't think that's a good idea, gets me off the treadmill."

"I know, but you should have time off. How was the weekend? Was your mom's new husband-to-be nice?"

"Actually, he's great."

"That's wonderful for your mother."

"It is. The wedding will be in June. I've marked it here on the calendar. I'll be off Thursday until Tuesday."

"All right. I'll make sure nobody can get to you."

"Thank you. I'd better call Fred. It's three o'clock over in Germany, isn't it?"

"About that." Alison went to the door. "I'll put the call through and buzz when he's on the line.

As soon as Alison was out of his office, Adam called home. Stella told him that Katy was sleeping peacefully. When he got back next week he'd arrange an audition for her. That would be a good way to see her again without making it seem personal.

•

By late afternoon Katy's headache had been replaced by a rather delicate, lightheaded sensation as she walked weakly into the bathroom to take a bubble bath that Stella had prepared for her.

When Katy was back in bed, she said, "I'm really sorry to give you extra work, Stella."

"I don't mind a bit." Stella patted the duvet. "I'll be serving a light dinner in the kitchen about six. You're welcome to join us."

"I'll see," Katy told her.

"You never know how you will feel later. And you don't have to rush away. You have the car until Saturday."

"I didn't need it until Saturday."

"Adam said Saturday. So I booked it until Saturday. It'll only be charged until you return it."

"I hope so. It's expensive." Adam must be thinking she was becoming a nuisance.

"Don't worry about it, Katy," Stella said.

With Stella gone Katy rested against the pillows plumped up against the headboard. Everyone said, don't worry, but she did worry. She worried about inconveniencing this household, and she worried about Adam and the burgeoning feelings she had for him. She also worried about her father marrying Adam's mother and the connection she would have with the Stevenson family for the rest of her life.

•

The worry didn't help the recovery of her headache. All her thoughts seemed to pound to the beat of the ache in her head. She was trying to sleep again when the door opened.

It was Jayne. The girl ran her hands down the sides of her denim shorts.

"Are you okay now, Katy?"

Katy wasn't quite sure if Jayne sounded concerned or merely felt obliged to ask the question because her father was away. "Not really," Katy said truthfully.

"Are you staying another night?"

Katy leaned on her elbow. "I'll have to."

Jayne's fingers ran down the door post. "That's fine. Dad would want you to stay until you were better."

"But you don't?" Katy hadn't meant to say the words, but they were out now. This visit to the Stevenson family home had been an intense strain from the minute she'd picked up the rental car on Friday afternoon.

She'd obviously made it worse for herself by her attraction to Adam, but she hadn't known he was the man she'd been dreaming about. Or that Adam himself would be so attractive. She wondered if she hadn't seen him leaving the limo that day if she would still have been attracted to him for the first time this weekend. She kind of thought she would've felt the same buzz.

Jayne said quickly. "I don't mind if you stay."

Katy let out a breath. "That's good. Because I'm not

well enough to drive home."

Jayne looked contrite. "I didn't mean for you to feel you had to leave. Are you coming for supper?"

Katy could see that while Jayne was very self-sufficient, she was also quite lonely. Katy decided to make the effort to eat dinner with her. After all, she wasn't going to lose her affiliation with Jayne by driving away from this house. They were going to be joined by family. And because of her own father's absence in her life around Jayne's age, she empathized with the girl. "Sure. I'll be there for supper."

"Okay. See you later."

After Jayne's visit, Katy thought the girl was jealous. Or maybe not so much jealous as frightened. Scared that her father might find someone who would take him away from her? Katy understood her feelings. She experienced a little of it with Trish. But as she was older and didn't live with her father anymore anyway, she couldn't really do much about her feelings. There came a time in life when you accepted relationships and her father and Trish's union was one of them for Katy. But even though Jayne had probably been exposed to many celebrities, she was still quite a sheltered teenager.

To try and regain some energy Katy washed her hair and blow-dried it until it tumbled over her shoulders. By the time she was dressed in jeans and a white cotton sweater, she decided she could face some food.

Katy hadn't been in the kitchen yet and when she walked in to the bright airy space, despite not feeling one hundred percent, she had to admire the room. Light shone from curved windows that seemed to have another patio outside with a table and chairs. The counters were butcher block, the appliances white, and the floor blonde hardwood. Jayne was sitting at a center island and Katy sat down on the stool next to her.

"This is a nice kitchen," she said.

"It is nice. We could eat outside if you like."

"No. This is fine."

"Anyway, you do look better," Jayne said. "Dad was very concerned about you. Probably because you're a guest and he felt guilty."

Katy moved a fork sideways on the cork placemat. She looked straight at Jayne. "Why should he feel guilty?"

"You got sick in his house."

"I often get migraines when I'm over-stressed, Jayne. It's nothing to do with this house."

The girl's lovely lips compressed. "Were you over-stressed this weekend then?"

Katy decided there were some things that needed to come out in the air between the two of them. "Yes. I was. My father re-marrying a year after my mother died isn't exactly what I expected."

Jayne didn't seem to anticipate that answer. "I thought you were stressed because of my dad."

Katy realized she was going to need to be diplomatic and probably fib a little. There was a tight lump in her throat. "Whatever gave you that idea?"

Jayne flushed. "I just thought—"

"Thought what?"

"That you liked him, or that he liked you."

"We got on okay so I guess we liked one another." Everything was becoming far more complex than merely a convergence of families. She looked forward to returning to the apartment, even if she did have to share it with Joe alone now.

Katy touched Jayne's hand on the counter. "Look. We should be friends."

Jayne smiled. "I guess. I'm not used to having anyone around much."

"Then let's have dinner together and enjoy ourselves."

•

Stella let Katy have anything she wanted. A bowl of chicken and rice soup, a small piece of grilled chicken and a tossed green salad was just what she fancied. But by the time she was finished, Katy realized she had used up all of her excess energy and she felt terribly tired. Jayne had some studying to do anyway. Katy thanked Stella for her help in getting her to her feet during the day and went back to her room.

Katy got into bed and used her cell phone to tell Joe why she wasn't home. He'd been worried but he'd had a great weekend with Heather.

The landline phone rang after she'd hung up. She wasn't sure whether this was a separate line or not and didn't bother answering until the ringing became insistent. It was Adam calling from Seattle.

Katy wished he hadn't called her. She just wanted to get out of this house and back to her life.

Adam said, "How are you feeling?"

"Much better. Thank you. Stella looked after me and I ate dinner."

"Great. Will you stay on until Wednesday?"

"Only if I can't move tomorrow."

"I would really like you to be there on Wednesday when I get home."

Katy didn't think that would be a good idea. She'd see him again at the wedding and she figured that might be enough for now. "I'm not sure, Adam. I'll see how I feel tomorrow. And while I've got you on the phone, I'll say, thank you for the weekend."

"Thank you. Take care, Katy."

On Tuesday morning Katy was well enough to go home. But she knew she would have gone home even if she'd still been ill. She needed to get away from Adam. Even when he wasn't here in his house she felt his presence surrounding her. Katy ate a subdued breakfast with Jayne, who rushed off afterward and returned to her room. She wore jeans teamed with her black suit jacket. When she was all set to leave with her car packed, she went back indoors to say farewell to Stella.

Stella said. "It's been a pleasure meeting you, Katy. I'm pleased you weren't sick for longer. I'll see you at the wedding."

"Are you going up?"

"My boyfriend, Jack and myself have been invited and we're going to take the opportunity to stay the rest of the week with Jack's daughter, who has a cottage at a lake in Muskoka. Adam has already agreed to that."

"It must be difficult getting a vacation with Adam's work schedule."

"Now that Jayne's older it's easier. But Jayne still gets left here alone a lot and now I understand she won't go up north for the summer as she usually does."

"No. Not with the wedding. I believe I heard that Molly Dean has invited her there instead." It had only been a comment she had overheard and she wasn't sure if she should become involved.

"Adam won't like that. He sees Molly as an influence on Jayne."

Katy frowned. "I don't understand why he's being so

stubborn with her about her music." Katy knew that she really shouldn't be speaking this way, but she felt that Jayne wasn't being listened to.

"Ah, well, that goes back a long way. You know who Jayne's mother was?"

"I do, yes."

"Well, Adam doesn't want Jayne going there. But he can't seem to see that she's not the same type of personality. Not that I ever met Rachel. What Adam needs is a steady woman in his life, then he'd be out of Jayne's way. But you'll learn the whole picture eventually, being family now."

But was she really part of the family? Katy asked the question as she drove back to Toronto. Stella was probably closer to family in a sense, because she had worked for Adam for such a long time.

Katy was pleased that Joe was still at work when she arrived home. She didn't feel like discussing her weekend quite so soon.

She dumped her luggage and went into the kitchen to find a soft drink. She discovered the kitchen neat and tidy. Heather's doing, no doubt. Joe wasn't as efficient. After taking a long drink, she kept the iced can in her hand and returned to the living room. It was smaller than Adam's foyer. Space was tightened by a number of stuffed book shelves, over-huge borrowed armchairs, a TV & stereo, crammed in between CD's and DVD's, and two desktop computers. There was also a laptop that Joe was using for music now.

Her piano took up a great deal of space. She hadn't touched it since Joe's band mates had moved it into the apartment for her. Although after playing Adam's piano she might be ready to begin again.

Adam. Then she told herself to snap out of this dream world. If she thought too hard about Adam, she would start looking forward to the wedding and begin building expectations again. Better to start getting her life back to normal. Therefore, she dragged her luggage into her bedroom and unpacked.

While she stored everything in its place once more, Katy realized her antique silver earrings were missing. Dismayed, she remembered Adam had removed them in the family room and slipped them into a dish. They were probably still there by the chair, where Adam had kissed her.

# Chapter Nine

When Adam arrived home on Wednesday he found Katy's room looking as if she'd never been there, tidy after Stella's cleaning. He stood staring at the neatly tucked-in bed. Even though she said she might not be here, he'd rushed home anyway. He walked desolately back to the kitchen, where Stella was preparing to leave now that he had arrived home.

"Your dinner's in the oven. I'll be back in the morning," Stella said, giving him a mischievous look.

"Thank you. Was she better when she left?"

"Katy?" The mischievousness persisted. "Yes. She was better."

Adam let out a taut breath. "Good."

Stella patted his arm. "Adam. Cheer up. Her address is on the counter on that notepad. I wrote it down from the car rental papers."

He felt immediately better. "Now why would you do that, Stella?"

"Because she's going to be part of your family."

"Of course," Adam said casually.

"There are also some silver earrings with the rental papers. They might belong to Katy. Jayne thought she remembered her wearing them."

He walked over to the counter and picked up the long earrings. They were an antique design and looked quite expensive. He could feel himself removing them from her ears, the way he'd slid the pad of each finger beneath her lobe and turned the small screw. "They might be," he said. "We were there on Saturday evening."

"They're not Laura's. I checked already and your mother wouldn't wear anything like that."

Adam rolled the earrings in his palm. "I want to make sure she's okay, so I'll take them with me and ask her."

"Well, I hope something works out for you. She is very nice. Now, do you want some dinner before I leave?"

Adam felt impatient that he couldn't be with Katy right away. He was even a little disgusted that Jayne wasn't home, when he actually had some spare time to be with her. He ate his dinner, saw Stella safely on her way, and then went to his study to make some phone calls. At nine he went to the gym, stripped into athletic shorts and began his exercise routine. He peddled furiously on the bicycle. He was figuring it was time to swim when Jayne came to the door.

"Hi, Dad."

He picked up a towel and scrubbed his face. "Where've you been?"

"I don't ask you that," she retorted.

"Yes. You do." She was wearing black flared pants and a tiny pink top under a long black jacket and she looked sophisticated. "Who were you out with?"

"Donna. We went to a mall shopping."

"Did you buy anything?"

"Jeans and stuff."

"Good." He decided to lighten up and smiled. "It's okay. I just wondered where you were."

"You didn't tell me you would be home tonight otherwise I would have left a note."

"I didn't know I would be home. I thought I might have to stay on but Lilah's recovering and can possibly continue the tour and return to the missed venues. Anyway, I expected you here."

"I don't wait home for you."

Adam placed his palm to his forehead. "What is going on?"

Jayne shook her head. "Nothing. With me. But since you've met Katy, you've changed."

"This has nothing to do with Katy."

She gave him a pointed look. "No?"

"Well maybe something," he said honestly, flipping the towel into the air. "Okay. So I liked her. Anything wrong with that? She's a cool looking woman."

"You really liked her?"

"I really liked her, honey. Be pleased for me, why not? I haven't really cared about a woman for a long time. Let me have the feelings."

He must have sounded really desperate because Jayne came over to touch his arm. "Are you sure you're okay, Dad?"

"Yeah. I'm fine, sweetie. I'm just going through a little crisis."

"I hope she doesn't hurt you, Dad. That's all."

Adam hoped so as well. He had been desperately hurt a few times but he'd always hidden the pain beneath the success of SMM.

When Jayne was gone he went through to the pool.

He slipped into the sultry water and began to swim hard and fast. He wasn't kidding himself about this new exercise routine. It felt like the first step to some sort of personal recovery.

After a restless night, Adam spent an equally restless morning at SMM, mostly in deadly boring meetings. He was pleased when he found Alison had arranged a financial meeting for the afternoon that would take him into downtown Toronto. He parked near the tall bank building, thinking, if the meeting was swift, he might be able to see Katy.

He walked into the meeting, his hand in the pocket of his leather jacket, his fingers fiddling with the piece of paper containing Katy's address and the little box containing her earrings. During a break in the meeting he called Katy's phone. There was no answer, no voicemail either, just incessant ringing into a hollow vacuum. He didn't know if she had a cell phone. And if she did he didn't know that number.

When the meeting was over, he drove to the address. He found it applied to a brick house that had been converted into two apartments. In front was a small overgrown fenced garden. The only available parking was on the crowded street, where cars sat both sides against the curbs. Adam had to cruise up and down the narrow street a few times before he found a space and even then he was only allotted an hour. He had to walk a couple of short blocks before he located the house. It was a narrow house with steps up to the front bright green door. He rang a bell and waited for a moment, then rang again. He glanced around the neighborhood. There were people around but no one next door either side.

"Looking for someone?" a male voice asked coming up the steps.

Adam saw the man wearing a charcoal business suit take a key from his pocket.

"I'm looking for Katy Kerr. Does she live here?"

"Yes. She does, but I believe she's out right now."

Adam gave the man a more intense stare. He had handsome features, dark eyes and slick hair. If this man knew where Katy might be and was now in the process of unlocking the door to Katy's apartment, then what did that actually mean? Did Katy live with this man? Hot jealousy flared up inside Adam but he tried for a cool smile. "She stayed at my place over the weekend. She left something behind and I'd like to give it to her personally. Maybe you can tell me where she is."

An expression Adam couldn't quite interpret crossed the man's face.

"Sure. She's at a restaurant called Veggie Things on Front Street. She doesn't actually work there, she's part-owner, but she helps out if they're busy." Joe dug in his pocket and pulled out his wallet. He passed Adam a card. "That's the exact address."

She hadn't told him she was part-owner of a restaurant. Adam took the card, slipped it into his pocket. "Thanks ..."

"Joe Mason."

"Adam Stevenson." They shook hands.

Joe said. "I'm pleased to meet you, Mr. Stevenson. I've heard about you. I'm a musician."

Adam's stomach muscles clenched harder. Another musician? "That's great, Joe. Nice to meet you as well."

Joe grinned. "Good luck finding Katy."

Adam was amazed that no questions had been asked

about his quest for Katy and he wondered if this was some kind of setup. Katy says to her boyfriend, if Stevenson ever comes to the apartment, be nice, we have a lot at stake.

Adam heard the door of Katy's apartment closing as he strode away. He climbed into his car and sat for a moment feeling a mixture of frustration, irritation, disappointment—all those things and more. He banged the steering wheel with his fist. She lived with a man who was a musician to boot. With this new knowledge, should he even bother trying to see her? He was going to have to see her again anyway at the wedding. But he knew he wouldn't be satisfied today if he didn't see her. Besides, he wanted to return the earrings, even though he could easily have handed them to Joe. He pulled out the card and put the address into his GPS.

He had to park the car and walk to Veggie Things. He was surprised how nice it was. The building was cleaned up red brick about four stories with arched windows on the second and third floors. There was a black iron fence, with flowers around it in pots and about four tables for outdoor dining. The door was black and he opened it.

He saw Katy right away. She was taking an order looking crisp and efficient in a pair of black pants and a white blouse. Her dark brown hair was confined upon her head with wispy bits down her cheeks. After she'd written down the couple's order and whipped the menus from the table, she looked up and saw him.

Adam saluted and saw a bright smile appear on her face. Encouraged by the smile, he moved to one of the red chairs at a square wooden table.

"Hi," she said, coming forward. "Joe called to say you

were on your way. Just let me put this order in. Do you want coffee or fruit juice?"

Joe had alerted her. Great! "Coffee's fine," he told her. She was very friendly because of what he could do for her or friendly because she genuinely liked him? Or her smiles could even be fake friendliness because he was a customer.

"House Blend?"

Adam nodded. "Sure. Double cream. Thanks."

He watched Katy at the bar putting in her orders. She hadn't lost any of the essence he'd found so appealing on the weekend. She was like a diamond. She always glittered. But for how many men?

She returned with a glass mug in a stainless steel holder and placed it in front of him. Then she went to get a small tray containing a tiny cream jug.

"Thanks. Do you have a moment?"

She perched on the opposite chair. "I didn't think I would see you again until the wedding."

"I wanted to see how you were." He reached in his pocket and pulled out the box. "You also left these behind."

She touched the box, tugged it forward and opened it. "Oh, my earrings. Thank you. They belonged to my mother. I think they were my grandmother's. They're antique."

"They're nice," he said. "I remember removing them."

Her eyes met his and he saw her mouth tremble. She hadn't forgotten their kiss. Neither had he. Except now Joe was in the picture and that made Adam feel bleak.

She touched one of the wisps of hair beside her delicate earlobe. She wore plain gold rings in her ears today, pierced, not the screw-on type like the old-fashioned silver earrings.

"I felt terrible about getting a migraine at your house."

Adam watched her fingers continue to fiddle with her hair. "It's not your fault. How are you feeling now?"

"Better. Thank you. Being able to sleep all day Monday fixed me up."

"You could've stayed longer."

"I stayed until Tuesday. Long enough. But how did you know where I lived?"

"The car rental agreement."

"Oh. Yes. I have to repay you for that."

"No. You don't. Count it as part of the weekend package."

She didn't argue. He picked up the cream jug, poured the contents into his coffee, and sipped the steaming liquid. The brew possessed an aromatic bistro flavor. "This is good."

"We're known here for our coffee."

He looked around. "This is a pretty classy building."

"We like it. Carol's my partner. The lady with the black hair."

Adam saw the woman behind the counter using an adding machine. "How long have you run the restaurant?"

"Four years."

"Have you ever had entertainment here?"

"Actually, no." Katy glanced around. "However, it might be an idea."

"It would help get your career going again?"

"You mean me perform here?"

"Of course. You could put a piano in the corner instead of the big plant."

"I never thought of that Adam. You're good."

"Seeing the possibilities is what I do."

She smiled and glanced around at the counter. "My order's ready. Excuse me."

Sipping the coffee, watching her serve the customers, Adam decided to ask her if she wanted to drive up to Hammond Lake with him for the wedding. Even if she did have a relationship with Joe, her father was still marrying his mother. That couldn't be altered. And if Joe was important, wouldn't she be bringing him to the wedding? Of course she might be for all he knew and he was sitting here waiting for the firing squad.

When Katy was finished, she poured a coffee for herself and sat down with him. "Carol will take over now."

"Does this place make money?"

"Oh, yes. We're in a great location, just along from Union Station."

"I noticed that." Adam turned his cup around on the table. She had a life and he wondered if he should or could be in it. "Do you want to drive up north with us, to the wedding?"

Katy's top teeth worried her bottom lip. She had beautiful even teeth. Adam couldn't get over how hard he was falling for her. It felt crazy. "Save renting another car."

"Okay," she said. "That would be fine."

At least he had that weekend clear with her. "Good. We'll make plans. I'll phone you about it."

"All right."

He took out his phone. "Do you have a cell number?"

She quoted the number and he entered it. He typed in her name. Now he would have constant contact with her. "What are you doing after you finish here?" he asked.

"Going home."

"How do you go home?"

"Bus. Subway. And I walk the last bit."

"Is that safe?"

"It's the way I travel. I'm used to it."

"How about tonight I pick you up?"

"It's a while yet." She glanced at the black framed wall clock. "I'm here until seven. I came in because one of our staff was ill."

"That's only just over an hour. I parked for half the night so I'll wait."

"Do you want something to eat then?"

"Okay. I'll see what you've got."

She handed him a slim black shiny menu.

He ordered a garden green salad and a cup of the broccoli and cheese soup with whole-wheat bread.

•

"He's deadly," Carol said in the back when Katy returned from serving a plate of greens to a customer. "The type of guy to make a woman dream."

"My soon-to-be step-brother," Katy said wryly.

"If we all had step-brothers who looked like him, what a heavenly world it would be. Mine's a twelve-year-old computer nerd."

Katy chuckled. Carol's mother had been married and divorced three times. The fourth marriage was to a younger man with a small son.

Carol said. "Did he make a move on the weekend?"

"We shared a kiss."

"Ah. He's interested."

"I know he's interested. I'm interested as well. But

there are some blockades to happiness."

"Like what?"

"He's a really busy man who hasn't got much time for anyone in his life."

"How do you know that?"

"He has a teenage daughter who doesn't get his attention."

"Oh dear. So where's his wife?"

"He never married. The girl's mother is dead." Katy didn't want to give away the identity of Jayne's mother. She was under the impression it was a guarded family secret. Although she was sure a lot of people knew who Jayne's mother was, at the moment no one had been indiscreet. She must remember to do a search on Joe's computer when she returned to the apartment.

"Well. At least there's no ex hanging around. That's a plus." Carol made a face. She was her husband's second wife and in the past had had trouble with the ex.

Katy grinned. "A big help. Let's put it this way, if I got involved with Adam it would be much deeper water than I've ever waded into."

"I know what you mean," Carol said.

But Carol didn't know the half of it, Katy thought as she finished helping tidy up before the two evening waiters arrived. Her hands trembled as she stood in the tiny washroom and took down her hair, brushed it, repaired her make-up and wished she was wearing something more alluring than the shirt and pants.

She pressed the heel of her hand to her forehead. She had never dated a man like Adam in her life. He was a man who could take her to heights emotionally and lower her into depths of despair when he dumped her. Not a smart move, Katy decided as she shrugged into the fitted jacket that matched her pants, grabbed her bag, said goodnight to Carol and met Adam where he was waiting outside on the sidewalk.

"So where's your car?"

"Walk with me, we'll find it."

She walked beside him on the sidewalk, side-stepping other walkers, thinking how good he looked in his black jacket over loose-styled slacks, a white shirt and a burgundy tie.

They came to the parking lot and she settled into his car. When Adam got in beside her, the leather jacket mingled with the leathery aroma of the interior. He buckled his seatbelt.

"Do you want me to drive you home?"

"Isn't that the intention?"

"We could go for a drink?"

Katy's eyes were drawn to the way Adam's hair splayed over his collar, a street light that had come on early despite daylight saving gleamed on the brown strands. She wanted to kiss him, to be held by him, to love him. But she said, "No. I don't think so. Thank you anyway."

He didn't start the car. "I want to ask you something about Joe Mason. Do you live with him?"

Adam's tone when he said, live with him, proved to Katy what he thought. "I don't live with him in the sense you're talking about."

"You don't share a bed with him?"

"Heaven's no. Joe and I have been friends for years. We went to university together. He's going to marry my friend, Heather, in September."

"Then why isn't he living with your friend? Why you?"

Katy disliked being questioned so forcefully about something so completely innocent. But she explained the situation anyway.

She sighed. "I was sharing with Heather when Joe moved in before they were to get married. They wanted to save money. Actually, I was going to move out so they could have the apartment after they were married. Then plans changed and Heather had to move back home with her mom so Joe and I were left together."

"Heather doesn't mind that you're alone with her boyfriend?" He still sounded edgy.

"No. It was her suggestion. I gave them space this weekend to be together, while I stayed at your house, which is why I couldn't go home until Monday." Katy saw that Adam's eyes seemed metallic blue in the dim lighting and she couldn't sort out what he was thinking. "You do believe me?"

"Yes. I do. However, Joe, your friend, mentioned he was also a musician."

"Oh, dear. Well, don't mind him. He works at a bank but his first love is music. He has a band. They usually get a gig each weekend. They've made a couple of CDs."

"Would you want me to help him if I helped you?"

"Of course not. And I don't want you to help me either, if you don't feel I have enough talent. I can manage on my own."

"I want to help you. I'm going to Germany tomorrow, but when I come back, we can work something out."

She couldn't take the pressure of an audition in the short time before the wedding. And what if he hated her voice or her music? The rejection would be between them at the wedding. "Why not after the wedding?"

"Okay. That gives me breathing space and you've got time to work up something to show me."

"Sounds fine to me," she said. Being with Adam was very much like driving fast on the wrong side of a road.

# Chapter Ten

Adam drove to her apartment, parked and walked her to the bottom of the steps to her door. "Is Joe home?" he asked, feeling, what was now a stab of jealousy whenever he thought about her room mate.

"I don't think so. He's usually with Heather."

"Okay then. Take it easy, Katy. I'll be in touch about the wedding trip."

"Thank you."

He leaned over to kiss her and felt her mouth respond as soon as his lips met hers. He could feel emotion well up inside him. *This is bad, Adam. Real bad.* He had been caught unawares. He wrapped his arms around her. It had been years since he'd stood on a pathway and kissed a woman, but he couldn't stop. Neither could she, because her fingers were stroking his hair and she was tucked deliciously against him. But they were out in the open and there was a streetlight not far away. Reluctantly he dropped his hands from her and stuffed his fists into his jacket pockets.

They stood looking at one another. He was sure her eyes were glistening with tears. "I'll miss you," he said, not really meaning to say that.

"Yeah, me too."

"See you then."

"Yeah." She gave him a little wave. "Have a safe trip."

"I will."

He walked down the path to the sidewalk and took one last look back at her before he went to his car. Two and a half weeks stretched like an eternity.

•

Katy waited for his car to take off. She watched the rear lights disappear down the road, a sinking sensation in her stomach. She swallowed back the tears. Miss him was an understatement.

Another car stopped near the curb and Joe climbed out.

"Hi." He pocketed his keys in his jeans. "Did Stevenson find you?"

She cleared her throat. "Yes."

Joe looked down the street. "Did I miss him?"

"He only brought me home."

"Only?"

They walked into the apartment together. Katy closed the door. She didn't put on the light.

Joe scratched his head uncertainly. "I was hoping something would be happening for you with Adam."

Katy felt the cloak of doom fall on her shoulders. It was like the day her father had called. *About your mother, Katy.*

"What?" she asked, hearing resignation in her voice.

Joe said quickly, "I'm thinking of moving in with Heather and her mother. We could save more money. Her mother thinks it's a good idea. She feels guilty for separating us and postponing the wedding. I really miss Heather being here all the time. The weekend you spent at Stevenson's proved it to us. We hate being apart."

Katy received the message loud and clear. "You mean you want to move out on me now?"

"Yep. But not until you get someone else to share. No hassle."

"Joe. It is a hassle. All my friends are either married or couples. This place is quite expensive."

"Then find somewhere else to live. You have that apartment above the restaurant."

"Carol and her husband are living there until their house is being built. Are you saying you're not going to live here with Heather when you're married?"

"We're going to buy a house instead. Her mother is going to help us."

"I see, so if you move out now, you're gone for good?"

Joe nodded.

Katy shrugged. She'd have the whole place to herself, which was appealing. "Okay. Move out. I can scrape up enough for the rent."

"Are you sure?"

"Yes. I'm sure." Katy was getting sick and tired of all her friends moving on to married life. She had a vision of herself being the aunt to all their children.

"The lease is good until the end of August. That gives you time."

"I guess, Joe. Fine."

"I'm sorry," Joe said and touched her shoulders.

Katy met his dark gaze, thinking about what Adam had insinuated and wondered if sex with her had ever crossed Joe's mind, whether it was crossing it even now. "Things might work out with Adam Stevenson."

"I doubt it," she said and pulled away from Joe. "It's okay. I'll survive."

"Isn't Stevenson going to at least help you with your career?"

"Later, after the wedding, I might audition."

"Well, then, hell, I'd be jumping around like crazy."

"It hasn't happened yet, Joe. Besides, it's complicated with our parents getting married. It's like I'm using the situation."

"What's wrong with that?"

"I have ethics."

"Screw the ethics." He smiled.

"No. I'm not. Adam is a nice man and he's a very serious businessman. I'd have to be top-notch to be taken on by SMM."

"You're good. You're a really terrific writer. He'll see that."

"I suppose he will."

"I don't know why you're so upset about him."

"I expect more than I ever get and I'm sort of wrung out emotionally. Oh, Joe, it's okay. Things will work out. Now, I'm tired and I'm going to bed." With more tears threatening, Katy abruptly left the living room and walked into her bedroom. She locked the door and lay down on the bed, thought about Adam, cried a little, and ached to see him again.

•

Adam looked at Fred Donaldson's tough leathery skin and watery blue eyes. He had hired Fred in the early days of SMM. At first Donaldson had been full of fire. But after two marriages and two divorces, and his children back at home in college, Fred wasn't as enthusiastic about SMM as he used to be. Half the time they didn't seem to understand one another any more and Adam wanted to fire his ass. But he knew he couldn't.

Fred was a friend and he eventually came through.

Adam patted the contract on the table. "Let's look at this before we go over to London tomorrow." They'd almost lost Kick Start to a UK management company and that mess had to be sorted out. The band was spinning its wheels in London. He couldn't blame the entire fiasco on Fred, but if Donaldson had been paying attention instead of trying to bed Darlene, who Adam had met last night, then he might have been able to save the situation.

They spent the rest of the afternoon sorting out the contract and went out for dinner with a couple of German business associates. The next day Adam flew to London with Fred. Adam slept in the plane and some of his dreams included Katy. When they landed at Heathrow he felt a hollow sensation in his stomach, which had nothing to do with physical hunger, because he had eaten a meal.

They had an immediate business meeting as soon as they reached their hotel. This led to a late night tour of some clubs. Their friends in London usually supplied women, but Adam wasn't interested in the blonde who tried to claim his interest. While he didn't sleep with any of these women, he always enjoyed taking a woman for dinner or a drink.

But this evening he couldn't seem to summon any interest for a date. By the time he reached his hotel suite and was alone he couldn't even recall her name. Katy was the only woman's name he remembered clearly. He reached for his phone and punched her number. It would still be evening in Toronto. Except there was no answer so he sent a text, something he rarely did.

*It's me, Adam in London. Coming home in time for the wedding. Text back please.*

In the morning there was a reply on his phone. *Looking forward to the wedding, L Katy.*

Did *L* mean *Love*?

•

Adam flew home from London a few days before the wedding and was met by his driver, Todd Freeman in the SMM limo at Toronto's Pearson Airport. Todd had been with him for ten years, a dark-haired man with a solid build, and not much sense of humor, but Adam trusted him. He was a good driver.

As they drove out of the airport in the mid-afternoon, Todd asked, "Where do you want to go?"

"Office please," Adam said, even if too many meetings and late nights, plus jet lag, made his eyes itch and left his face full of stubble. He called Jayne, while he shaved with his battery razor.

"Dad it sounds like you're mowing the lawn in my ear."

"My face looks like the lawn, sweetie and feels just about as green. How's home?"

"Running smoothly. I saw Katy."

His heart flipped. "You did?"

"Yeah. We're going to be bridesmaids and we all went shopping in Toronto with Grandma to buy dresses."

"Did you get dresses?"

"We did, and we had lunch. Laura was there as well. You're going to be the usher so you have to dress up. I've looked through your stuff and picked out a suit."

"Good. Have you been going to school?"

"I'm finished now, Dad. I'm on my gap year. My music year."

"Yes. Didn't you have grad?"

"Weeks ago, don't you remember. I went with Justin."

"Yeah." He figured he'd forgotten grad because he wanted to forget Justin, with his wide footballer's shoulders, floppy hair and bedroom eyes.

"Anyway," she said, "the weather should be perfect for the wedding on the weekend."

"Super."

"Are you coming home?"

"After I've been to the office."

"Fine. I have no more time to talk, Dad. Molly's here. Her parents are home. Bye."

Adam disconnected feeling very alone as the limo slid into the parking lot of SMM and dropped him off outside the door.

"Transfer my luggage into my car, please Todd," he said.

The driver nodded. "Will do."

He walked into the building and went to his office.

"Why did you come in here today?" Alison asked. "You look like you should have gone home to bed."

Adam sat down behind his desk. Alison had put all the work into tidy piles but it still appeared chaotic. He indicated the work with a nod of his head. "To check in."

Alison made a face. "You'll wish you didn't."

"Why?"

"Rory's back and adamant about giving up music and raising his goats."

Adam grimaced. "He has another album on his contract. Doesn't he realize that?"

Alison grinned. "Probably. That's could be why he's

procrastinating. Now you don't want to deal with Rory this week, Adam. You have the wedding to look forward to. Why don't you just go home and forget about this place until next Tuesday morning?"

"Tuesday. I'm off to where?"

"New York."

"All right," he said. "I'll go home. And then tell everyone else I'm in Asia."

Alison nodded. "Go. I can't stand you any longer."

Adam made his way out of the back entrance of SMM. Before he climbed into his car, he took off his suit jacket and loosened his tie. It was hot. When he reached the road, he sat at the intersection for a while trying to decide what to do. *Go to Katy. Go home to Jayne.* He called Katy. Why did she always have her cell phone turned off? And the apartment phone didn't have an answering service. Anyway, he was seeing Katy later this week anyway. He would phone her again to cement their plans when he reached home.

Stella had left early. There was a scrawled note from Jayne in his study telling him she had gone to spend the night with Molly, but promised to be back in time to prepare for the wedding. She was packed and ready.

Adam removed his tie as he walked wearily upstairs. Didn't his mood remind him of a Friday a few weeks ago, the day he'd met Katy for the first time?

He entered his bedroom, picked up the phone and sat down on the side of the bed. Katy's home phone rang and rang and finally he hung up. Why didn't they get voicemail? Or was it an omen for him to cool things with Katy? He sent her a text telling her that he'd pick her up at noon on Thursday. He was nearly asleep when he heard her text come in. He read it and then lay awake feeling extremely dissatisfied.

All she'd said was, "Okay, see you at noon."

# Chapter Eleven

Seeing Adam standing on her step wearing a pair of khaki pants and a white golf shirt, after what seemed like a very long absence, made Katy feel emotionally weak and unusually shy. Especially when his glittery gaze took in her black tank and cropped jeans with an interest that was purely male. She remembered how jealous he'd been of Joe.

"I'll be with you in a few seconds," she told him.

He stepped inside. "Take your time. It's not illegal to park outside, is it?"

"No. But you'll want to get a move on. The traffic might be bad going up north. The weather is so good everyone will want to go to their cottages."

"Don't worry about it. I'll be driving." He glanced around. "This place looks emptier."

"Yes." She pulled on a white silky shirt. "Joe moved out. He's living with Heather at her mother's house. It's a huge home. They're going to buy a house."

"So he's gone for good?"

"Yes." She smiled. "Does that make you feel better?"

"Relief," he said with a grin.

She slipped her leather purse strap over her shoulder and closed up the apartment. Adam moved ahead of her down the steps carrying her suitcase.

Jayne, wearing slim jeans, a blue top, with her hair in a pony tail, was waiting by the car.

"Hi, Jayne," Katy said, while Adam went to store her bags away.

Jayne slid into the back seat, leaving the front passenger seat available for Katy.

Not wanting to place an intentional wedge between father and daughter, she said, "Sure you don't want to sit beside your father?"

"No. I'm fine here."

Katy sat in the front and fixed her seatbelt.

Adam came to join them and started the engine. "Ready for take off."

"Zoom," Jayne said.

And Katy laughed.

Jayne leaned forward and placed her arms between the head rests. "Grandma took all our clothes up north with her. Dad, we got these really cool sheath dresses in an ivory color and leather high heeled sandals, really expensive, to match."

"Sounds good," Adam said.

"They're pretty," Katy said.

Jayne poked her father in the shoulder. "You must relax this weekend Dad. You know, Donna's father's friend he works with had a heart attack and he's only your age."

"I don't plan on having a heart attack."

"But you could, Dad. Grandma and Aunty Laura worry about you. You never let up."

Katy glanced at Adam. The edges of his mouth were slightly pinched, as if he were under a great deal of strain. She figured he must have jet lag. Luckily Jayne was there to keep the conversation flowing.

The traffic was stop and go upon leaving the city as everyone streamed north to the lakes. It would have been a terribly hot drive without the air-conditioning in the car. After a tense, traffic-filled highway drive, they stopped at a restaurant on the edge of the town of Barrie. Barrie was located on the shores of Lake Simcoe and Katy always thought of it as the northern border of Southern Ontario. From there on they would be in the part of the province, where winters were harsher and the summers slightly cooler.

In the restaurant, Jayne wanted to share a booth, so Katy pushed in beside her. She certainly didn't want to tuck herself against Adam.

"Smile, Dad," Jayne said after they were all served with glasses of iced tea. "It's vacation time."

Adam gave her a forced bright smile. "How's that?"

"Better."

They all ate salads, chicken fingers and plum sauce, which turned out to be Jayne's favorite food as well as Katy's. As they discovered this in common, she caught Adam glancing at them.

"Let's go to the drug store," Jayne suggested to Katy as soon as they were outside and Adam was still paying for their meal.

Katy glanced at the restaurant door. "Your father might want to get going."

"He can wait. It's taken this long to get here. It's not far now anyway."

"You better tell him."

Jayne ran back into the restaurant and Katy wondered if she'd get shot down over the shopping, but she came out a few seconds later with a big smile on her face and holding a wad of twenties.

"Permission granted. Let's go."

The store was packed with goodies claiming Jayne's immediate interest: Lipstick, nail polish, eye liner, foundation. She chose a pale color to match their wedding outfits.

"Laura once took an esthetician course and she will do our nails," she said.

She then scoured the book and magazine racks and selected a teen magazine with Molly Dean on the cover, a couple of romance novels, and a science fiction novel, books that Katy wouldn't mind reading herself. She doubted whether Adam even knew what books his daughter read. At the women's personal hygiene shelves, Jayne removed a couple of packages and placed them in the basket.

She looked at Katy rather shyly. "This is something Dad doesn't know."

"He knows," Katy said. "Men don't not know. They just aren't that interested because it doesn't affect them."

Jayne laughed. "I've never actually said anything to him. Laura helped me at the time."

Katy felt sorry for Jayne. But, even her own mother had been shy herself, and Katy had learned most things from girlfriends. She couldn't recall anyone ever sitting down with her and explaining what would happen to her body. She sympathized with Jayne about being brought up by a father. Since her own mother's death, Katy had come to realize how little interaction she'd had with her father since her childhood.

They reached the check-out counter and Jayne added a package of gum, a roll of mints, and a chocolate bar to her purchases. "What chocolate do you like?" she asked Katy.

"What you have is fine."

Jayne generously slipped another bar on to the counter and she looked at Katy in a friendly way. Katy smiled back her thanks. She liked Jayne and wanted to be friends with her.

•

Adam loosened his shoulders before he started the car. His daughter was right. He needed to relax more if he were to survive this weekend. However, as they climbed north from Barrie into cottage country, where the air wasn't quite as hot and humid as it was down in the south part of Ontario, he did feel the pressure inside his stomach subside and he felt less like he was growing an ulcer.

Rain spotted the windshield and the evening became dull, almost dark. Adam turned on the headlights and the wipers. Katy was silent, seemingly content to watch the scenery, and Jayne had fallen asleep.

Adam was pleased about the silence for he felt rather nostalgic about Hammond Lake. The house had belonged to his mother's parents and had been inherited by his mother. Trish Stevenson had eventually sold up her posh downtown condominium apartment and moved north to live.

Adam had spent a lot of his childhood here, swimming with Laura and the neighbor's kids, picking berries in the heat, arising in the morning to the sparkle of the lake and the fragrant aroma of bush and fresh water that he found, after many years traveling around the world, defined Canada for him.

Katy stirred and he turned to look at her. He had

tried to avoid too many long looks at her today as Jayne was with them. But now, with Jayne asleep in the back seat, he let his gaze roam over Katy. Her hair was ruffled from leaning her head against the headrest and he thought she appeared younger and quite fragile.

"Are we almost there, Adam?" she asked.

He reluctantly returned his attention to the road. "About another ten miles."

Katy sat up straighter. "When did your mom buy this property?"

"She didn't. She was born here. My grandmother on my mother's side was a Hammond and the house was built back in the eighteen hundreds. When my Grandparents were married they lived here. My mother inherited the property, but rented it out for a long time."

Katy made a sound of surprise. "I never realized it was a family home. No wonder she lives here then. My father owned a cottage not far from here and that's how they met. Did you know she originally met my dad in university? Apparently they barely acknowledged one another at the time, and went on to marry our respective parents. They met again recently and their romance is the result. I thought that story made their marriage not so sudden."

Adam hadn't known. He felt slightly guilty about that omission, for if he'd spent more time with his family, he would have. "She only told me that she'd met him at a golf club."

"Golf will certainly keep them together," Katy told him with a laugh.

This time, instead of keeping himself aloof from Katy, Adam let her laugh affect him the way it had from the moment he'd set eyes on her. Learning of their parents' connection gave them a connection. Not that he hadn't felt a connection from the moment he met her. "Do you think we had a destiny as well?"

"Maybe," she said in a whisper, with a glance over the backseat.

"It sure seems like it," he said softly, wishing they were alone. If they were he'd stop the car and kiss her.

He cornered a bend in the tree-lined road. A few moments later, Adam drove the car through double wooden gates and into the parking area. Other cars were parked there. The guests' swirling forms behind the lit windows emanated a steady hum of sound. Even though he knew he shouldn't make this wedding a chore, Adam sighed inwardly. For the next few days, he was resigned to being the dutiful son. The wedding weekend had begun.

. 

Katy had expected a small cottage, not a full size house. Outside lights illuminated pale blue siding and the porch dripped with Victorian lace overhangs. The square foyer was brightened by a chandelier sending sparkling prisms around the walls and down on to the polished wood floors. Stairs leading up from the foyer were covered with thick piled, dark blue carpet. The house had obviously been modernized but the original concept had been kept.

"It's a super house," Katy said to Jayne, while Adam placed their luggage to one side of the square foyer.

Jayne nodded. "I think it's awesome. But I was scared here when I was a kid. It creaks when it's windy."

"Let's hope it doesn't get windy," Katy remarked.

Trish left the party to greet them, looking attractive in a pale mauve dress. "There are goodies and drinks in the living room," she said. "Do you all want to go to your rooms first?"

"I'd like the goodies and drinks," Jayne said. "I'm starved."

Adam chuckled. "You stuffed yourself with chicken fingers on the way up here. How can you be starved?"

Jayne rolled her eyes. "Easy. I'm always starved."

"I wouldn't mind a visit to my room," Katy admitted.

Trish nodded. "Fine. Adam will take you up. It's the blue room for Katy overlooking the lake. You're next door, Adam, in the green room."

"Can I come to the party dressed this way?" Jayne asked.

"Of course you can, love." Trish placed her hand on Jayne's shoulder. "Come on. I've loads of people for you to meet."

Trish and Jayne disappeared into the party. Adam picked up the luggage once more.

Carrying her lightest bag and Jayne's small one, Katy followed Adam up the steep stairs. The second floor was less spacious than the first. Closed doors lined a narrow hallway and showed off the age of the home.

"Has the upstairs been renovated?" Katy asked.

"A few of the rooms, but the narrow hallway seemed to be a problem to change up here."

"Likely the house would fall down if you did change it."

"Possibly. I used to play train along here."

Imagining Adam as a little boy playing train was rather endearing. "How did you do that?"

"I took all the chairs from all over the house and set them up in twos facing one another. I'd be the conductor."

"Sounds like fun, Adam."

"It was fun." He tapped a door open and stood aside. "This is the blue room."

He left his and Jayne's luggage outside and placed Katy's bags on the floor beside the double bed. Snuggled upon the Iris blue duvet was a black and white cat.

"That's Jinx. The brown tabby you'll find down at the party cadging food is Monster. Jinx, meet Katy."

The cat's glowing eyes peered at Katy. Sensing a stranger, the animal suddenly dove off the bed, scampered across the blue carpet, and out of the blue door into the hall.

"She doesn't like me," Katy said.

"She'll get used to you. She's the flighty one."

"Has your mother always had these cats?"

"Since she returned to live here. They were strays."

"Neat. My mother was very particular about her home and would never allow animals inside."

Adam raised an eyebrow. "Except the human kind?"

"She was even particular about them as well. Shoes off at the door, no slouching on the cushions that type of thing."

"My mother was the opposite. We could do pretty much what we wanted."

"Cool," Katy said and wondered if her father found Trish's easygoing nature appealing after her uptight mother. Her mother's prissy attitude to everything in general had certainly sent Robert fleeing home as soon as he was able. Katy had been thrilled when she moved into her first apartment with three friends and there was the freedom to do what she wanted to do.

"Room okay?" Adam asked.

She glanced around. The room was aptly named.

The furniture was painted antique blue and the walls were forgetmenot blue with some flower stencils. "It's very pretty."

"Familiar?"

"A similar design to the room I stayed in at your house." Reminding herself of that weekend put a breathless lilt into her voice.

"Observant. Same interior designer, who is a friend of mother."

"It's great. Really great." Katy walked to the window.

"Like the view?"

Adam was right behind her at the window. Katy placed her hands on the window ledge and looked outside. Stone steps were illuminated by a row of lanterns. At the bottom was a swimming pool built into rock. "That's lovely."

"My grandfather built that pool. It's fed naturally."

Katy could feel Adam's breath close to her face and her fingers clenched. "So it's not chlorinated?"

"No. It's lake water. Down by the dock the lake is very deep. Better for boating than for swimming."

Katy moistened her lips before she spoke again. "We went to our cottage quite a bit. I enjoyed that. My mother wasn't quite so fussy at the lake. Even so, your mother is much more tolerant."

"Your mother couldn't have been very old when she died."

"No. She was only fifty-six."

"How did she get so uptight?"

"I think it's because her parents were very strict with her when she was young. They didn't let her date."

"How did she meet your dad then?"

"Through her parents. He was the son of someone

they knew." She shrugged. "Sometimes, the way she told the story, the relationship sounded arranged, but she did love him. Although, I have to be honest and say I wonder about his feelings. As soon as she died, he began to get rid of all her possessions."

"That's why you queried his feelings for my mother?"

She nodded. "But I saw immediately he was different with your mother."

"That's good. I only want my mother to be content."

"I know."

Adam stepped away from her and turned to the door. "I suppose we should show our faces. I'll meet you downstairs."

Katy nodded. "Fine."

He seemed to want to say more, but didn't, and left by closing the door firmly behind him.

Katy unpacked a few things and hung them in the closet. She saw all her wedding attire was already here, the high heeled sandals on the floor beneath the dress.

After fixing her hair and make-up and putting on a black linen skirt and a cream top, Katy finally went downstairs to join the party. She congratulated her father and Trish, checked in with Jayne who had found a young man she knew, and then began to meet new people. Lana, a lovely silver haired lady, who'd been Trish's friend since childhood, her husband, Garth, a lawyer, and the list went on until Katy's head whirled with new names and faces.

In between she nibbled snacks she knew her stomach could do without. Sensing a great source of extra food, Monster, the tabby began to trail her around and she crouched to pet him and feed him some cheese.

"Found a pal?" Adam said.

Katy rose to her feet. "Yep. He obviously knows a light touch when he sees one. I love cats."

"That's good because you'll probably be bugged by him for the rest of the weekend."

Someone came up to speak to Adam and Katy took her chance to leave the party.

Upstairs, Jinx was on her bed again and Katy sat down and ran her hand over the cat's luxuriously soft fur. This time, Jinx purred and didn't run away.

# Chapter Twelve

Adam was up early because he hadn't slept particularly well with Katy in the room next door. He quickly zipped his jeans and stuffed his socked feet into athletic shoes, pulled on a black sweatshirt, raked his fingers through his hair, and quietly closed the door to his room. He left the house by the back door off the second level. After going down the wooden stairs, he circled the deck, crossed the patio, and took the stone stairway to the pool. He passed the pool and continued to the lakeshore. A wooden dock stretched from the boathouse upon the calm glassy water but Adam chose the footpath that would take him beside the rocky edge of the lake.

He walked at a good clip, trying not to think past the glorious scent of the early morning, with the mist rising off the water and the sky promising to be a hard blue. When he reached the road, he jogged along the gravel surface, the added adrenaline giving him an outlet for his inner turmoil that was mostly over what to do about Katy. He wanted to be alone with her today, but he knew his mother would have a list of chores for him over the weekend to keep him occupied. Just the thought of all he would have to do, which would probably leave no time for Katy, made him run faster and faster until he arrived back at the cottage worked into a lather of a sweat.

He entered by the kitchen door. Laura was there.

"Hey, big brother," his sister said. "Where have you been?"

Adam placed his hand on the counter, lowered his head, and breathed deeply. "Around the lake and up the road."

He accepted a glass of water from Laura. "Thanks."

"Pleased to see you relaxing," his sister told him. "Now go get cleaned up. Big day ahead of us."

He showered, shaved and dressed in clean jeans and a golf shirt then returned to the kitchen. Katy was there now in shorts and a white top. So was Jayne and they were chatting amiably as they prepared breakfast for anyone who came through. They made him some rye toast and poured him coffee. When he'd eaten Jayne wanted him to string colored lights all over the property. After the lights were hung he was designated to drive Jayne into the closest town to pick up some last minute supermarket items.

"This is fun, Dad," Jayne said as he drove the dusty gravel road back to the house.

"It's hectic. I'm not sure about fun."

"Don't be such an adult."

They arrived back at the house to find Katy's brother, Robert, his wife, Patty, and the two boys, Tobin and Stuart had arrived. They were a pleasant enough family. Robert looked like a younger version of Paul, Patty was full-figured and dark-haired, and the boys were boisterous. The commotion added yet another barrier between him and Katy, and Adam began to get frustrated with the situation. Even though he took on a lot of responsibility himself at SMM, he still only had to snap his fingers and assistants and staff moved for him. Today his control was out of control.

His mother bustled into the kitchen. "Did you get everything, Adam?"

He closed the fridge door on the final purchase. "Everything on the list and more that Jayne decided we might need."

"Good. Everyone is here. So now we're going to have some lunch. We have to feed Paul's family." His mother frowned. "You're really not in a good mood at all, are you?"

Adam leaned his hips against the counter top and crossed his arms over his chest. "I'm okay. I'm just winding down from work. I was in England a few days ago."

"It's not just this last trip you're winding down from, Adam. You haven't been yourself for months now, maybe even years." Trish shook her head. "Adam. You need a girlfriend. How about Katy? She hasn't got a boyfriend. I thought you two hit it off well that weekend at your place, but last night I noticed you weren't together."

He couldn't explain Katy to his mother. He couldn't even explain his feelings to his own brain. "This is your weekend."

"I know, but I can't be worried about you all the time."

"I'm a grown man. There's nothing to worry about." Adam decided he had to change his attitude. If it was acting a lie, then so be it. He forced a chuckle. "Please enjoy yourself."

"I do intend to." Trish moved forward and peeled a white thread off of Adam's golf shirt and balled it between her fingers. "Can I ask you a favor then? We'll be gone a month to Bermuda. Somebody will come in and check this house, but I'll need the cats looked after. You wouldn't mind, would you, Adam?"

He'd had them a few times. "Take them back with me, you mean?"

"Yes." Trish kept balling the piece of thread. "We intend to travel quite a bit."

Adam lifted an eyebrow. "You want me to keep them forever?"

"Jayne loves them and it'll be good for her. She needs something. You both need something. You live in some sort of a vacuum. All that secrecy and privacy over her mother isn't healthy."

"I don't want Jayne to be hounded by the press."

"I understand that, but it's probably common knowledge and one day someone will say something and you'll have to be prepared for that. Personally, I don't think Jayne will care."

Adam shook his head. "But not this weekend. Please."

"I just wanted to talk to you before I get married and I won't see you quite so much. Let Jayne do what she wants to do and get a life. Isn't that what they say these days?"

Adam sighed. "Okay. I agree. I need a life."

"At least you know what I'm talking about." His mother shook her head. "You don't realize how much you miss when you don't have a partner until you have one again."

*Probably true*, Adam thought, although in retrospect he'd never actually had a truly intimate partner.

"You know what I mean, Adam?"

"I know what you mean. But don't worry about me. Take your own happiness. It hasn't been easy for you either."

"You were always such a great help to me when your father left that I don't like to see you suffering."

"I'm not exactly suffering."

"I know, but you have to buck up. You'll be forty before you know it."

His mother left him with that grim reminder. He went to the fridge for a cold beer, popped the top and took a swig.

"A secret drinker?" his favorite female voice said.

Finally, face to face with Katy, Adam lifted the bottle. "Want some poor man's champagne?"

"I certainly would." Katy fanned herself with her fingers. "There's a cool breeze off the lake, but it's still warm. The boys wanted to play Frisbee so we had to go out front to the lawn."

He handed her an opened beer. "Do you need a glass?"

"No. The bottle is fine. It tastes better." She took a sip and licked her lips. "That's good. Thanks."

For once Adam felt he actually had time to be with her. He didn't have to move from this house until Sunday. So he let his gaze travel from her bare feet in white canvas shoes, up her long legs, to the edge of her shorts beneath her T-shirt. "I like your hair in a braid."

She touched the braid and brought it over her shoulder. "It's quite breezy up here. I thought it would be a neater way to control my hair. I also want to swim later."

He kept his gaze locked with hers as he filled up with

even more heat.

She looked at him rather boldly and raised an eyebrow.

"It happens when we're together," he said. "I can't help it." He put out his hand.

With a slight hesitation she placed her fingers into his. He drew her toward him, kissed her damp mouth, felt her respond and eased a thigh between hers. She tucked her legs closer to his and Adam let himself escape into the feelings and the heat. He put his bottle down behind him on the counter, took hers from her wavering hand, and with his palms against her behind, he pulled her to him. With a groan he eased himself into a sensuous kiss.

"Excuse me."

It was Katy's brother, Robert. Feeling very dazed, Adam released Katy.

Katy picked up her beer and tossed her braid over her shoulder. "Robert. Do you want a beer?"

"I wouldn't mind." Adam saw him give his sister a crooked look. "I'll get it."

Robert, wearing a T-shirt, golf shorts and black and lime green rubber sandals that flapped at the heels, shuffled to the refrigerator, took out a beer, then went to a cupboard to look for a glass.

Adam glanced at Katy and saw she was actually trying to control her amusement. He smiled, but his smile turned into a grin until he had to actually force himself not to laugh out loud.

Robert poured his beer very carefully sideways into the glass. "Never let Katy ever pour you a beer, Adam," he said. "She does it carelessly and you get more foam than beer."

"I'll remember that," Adam said, trying to dilute the humor in his tone. He lifted his bottle. "I'll stick to drinking from a bottle when I'm around her."

With his beer perfectly poured into the glass, Robert lifted the empty bottle. "Do you recycle these?"

"Put them in the box," Katy said. "We'll take them back to the beer store."

"Oh, yes." Robert slipped the bottle in the box, shuffled back to the table, picked up his glass and nodded. "Well, continue."

They both burst out laughing. They laughed so hard they had to sit down at the kitchen table. Adam reached for Katy's hands across the table.

Then they began laughing again until they were aching.

"I shouldn't laugh. He's my brother."

"He's nothing like you."

"That's true. Although he escaped her, he has hints of my mother in him. I think he's going to be a real prissy old man."

The humor ebbed and they looked at one another more seriously. "So what happens now?" Adam asked. "Each time we've kissed it felt so good."

Katy stared down at their joined hands. "When I finished my last relationship, I vowed never to have expectations again. I thought I could go with the flow. But I'm not sure that's going to work. I need to have some expectations. I need some direction."

"You don't think I can offer you that at all, do you?"

"Do you?"

He squeezed her fingers. "I don't know, Katy. When I'm away from SMM it seems easy enough. I'm here with you now. We have time to be together. But when I enter the office, or I'm on a plane somewhere, I'm gone."

"You like that life, don't you? You must."

"I did. Although, I have to admit, I'm really weary."

"I can see you are."

"But when I'm with you, Katy, I lighten up a lot. You must notice that."

"So what am I supposed to be, Adam, your relaxation toy?"

He didn't smile because that's just about what she might become if they continued this way. "I don't know."

She let go of his hands and rose from the table. "I think I'll leave you to figure out what's going to happen. I'm willing to enter into a relationship with a future. But that's all." She slipped her empty bottle into the box.

"And there's more to it than just you and me. It's the parents as well, and Jayne. We have to be sure. Anyway, I'll see you later."

·

After lunch, the entire family organized a volleyball game in the pool. Katy didn't want to play, so wearing shorts and a top, she watched Adam from behind her dark glasses. When he was having fun, he became less formidable. Although why he should be formidable now she knew him in a more familiar setting she wasn't sure. Possibly because he was still, and would always be, Adam Stevenson, maker or breaker of musicians' dreams. If she wasn't a musician herself, would she feel differently about him? She lay back on the lounger and closed her eyes until drops of water splashed on to her stomach.

"Don't like volleyball?" Adam asked, sitting down on the ground beside her lounger.

"Not particularly. You're wet." Katy tossed a towel at

him.

He rubbed his hair and she loved his tousled look.

"Let's escape," he said.

"Where to around here?"

"The dock."

She rose from the lounger and tucked her feet into her canvas shoes.

Adam pulled on a T-shirt and led the way down the rocky steps. The dock was around a bend hidden from the house by some big pine trees, so they weren't observed. Katy followed Adam to the end. The water below looked deep and cold.

"Did you ever swim here?" she asked him.

"Yes. We had a dog named Sheldon at one time who loved the water. Laura and I would jump in and we would yell and wave until Shelley dashed in to save us. Then we'd all have a great old time splashing."

"Was your dad here then?"

"In those days he was. He has a family album of photographs of all of us up here."

"Why did they break up?"

Adam shrugged. "I think he had an affair. I don't know for sure. Mom's never actually spoken about the reason. I'm not even sure if there was a concrete reason. I do know he didn't always have a steady job. There were some uncertain times. That's why it was so convenient to send his family up here for the summer with our grandparents. When Dad was here as well, we knew he was unemployed."

"Wasn't he a photographer?"

"That came later out of the unemployment."

"He should've done that from the beginning."

"You're right. I think that was another problem, he

didn't follow his dreams when he was young. Anyway, in the end, it worked out well for him."

"And it's worked out well for your mother."

"Yeah." A rush of wind off the lake made Katy step back and Adam placed his arm around her shoulders. He bent and kissed her mouth. "Let's not worry about any of the problems this weekend. Let's just take moments when we can."

And then he'll be gone again.

"Here they are, Dad," a boy's voice squealed.

"Careful on that dock. It doesn't look that safe," Rob shouted to his sons.

Katy smiled at her nephews. She'd been caught by her brother again.

"The dock is quite safe, Rob," Adam said, not removing his arm from around Katy's shoulders. "However, the water is deep at the end."

The boys spread on their stomachs and leaned over the edge.

"Are there fish in here?"

"Yes," Adam told them.

"Did you fish?"

"When I was your age."

"Can we fish?"

"I'm sure there are some rods in the boat house. Why don't we look?"

Adam released her shoulders and Rob and Adam went to look for fishing gear. Katy stayed with the boys.

Even Katy got a fishing rod and the five of them spent the rest of the afternoon on the dock. Nobody caught anything, but they had a lot of fun. Adam was patient and very helpful with the boys. She thought it was because he remembered exactly how being a boy felt. She wouldn't have thought any of this about him when she first met him. At that time she had seen only a cool, high-powered executive. Now she was beginning to see him as a man she could really fall in love with.

# Chapter Thirteen

Katy awoke on the wedding day to a bright sunny morning. She jumped out of bed and almost yelled with pleasure. She felt healthy. She felt good. She felt great.

She also felt energetic, so she drank a glass of water, put on sweat pants and a long-sleeved cotton top to ward off any insect life, and left the house by a side door off the kitchen. The air was wonderfully fresh and quite crisp, especially after the soggy heat in Toronto.

"Up early?"

It was Adam, dressed in sweats. He hadn't shaved yet and his jaw was shadowed and she thought he looked quite devastating.

"It's really great out here in the morning," she said.

"Walk with me then."

They began walking side by side. Adam stayed silent and Katy didn't break his commune with nature. But he walked fast and she was actually puffing when they reached the road and she realized they had a long way to go back to the house.

"Can we slow down for a moment?" she asked.

He gave her a concerned look and reached for her hand. "Hang on to me."

Katy felt an energy being transferred from Adam through their hands. Between them there was something more than mere physical attraction, she decided. This was something special. At least it was for her.

In the kitchen Laura, wearing a white silk lounge outfit, was pouring herself a mug of coffee.

"Hi, you two," she said. "Is it nice outside today?"

"A fantastic wedding day," Katy told her, realizing she was still holding Adam's hand, which had obviously prompted Laura's, you two.

"Good. Mom's just so happy. I'm pleased for her. Help yourself to coffee." Laura gave them both a smug look and left the kitchen.

Adam opened the refrigerator and took out a carton of orange juice. He poured two glasses of juice. Then he rested his hips on the counter. "Did you notice Jayne with Greg Carson last night?"

"A very handsome boy."

"He's okay."

Katy heard Adam's concern. "Oh, oh. Dad doesn't want his daughter to have a boyfriend."

"It's not that, Katy. I just want her to have some life before she gets tied down."

"She'll do whatever she wants, Adam. Don't mess her around. Let her grow up normally. Besides, he's probably only this weekend's flavor. She'll have lots of crushes."

"I hope you're right."

"Of course I'm right. Now I'm going to get showered and changed."

•

Katy went down for breakfast that was being served on the porch. There was no sign of the bride or groom, and the conversation mainly became a list of Laura and Adam's reminiscences from when they were children here.

When the meal was cleared away, Laura, Katy, Jayne and Trish went to the bedroom that had been set up as a beauty room. Laura painted all their fingers and toes with the polish to match their dresses then worked on their hair and makeup.

"I thought you had a child minders business," Katy said, when she looked at herself in the mirror with her perfect makeup and upswept hairdo.

"I trained as a beautician first," Laura said, moving to Jayne's hair. Trish was ready and had gone to her room. "You're very good," Katy said. "I look great."

"She always fixes me up," Jayne said. "She used to do Lilah Payne's hair before performances."

Katy smiled. "So you have worked with Adam?"

"Occasionally." Laura said.

Katy watched Jayne's hair and makeup change her appearance. "You're beautiful," Katy said. "Your Dad won't recognize you."

Jayne strapped on the high heeled sandals and stood in front of Katy.

Laura patted her niece's arm. "Your dad will realize you're grown up today. Now I'm going to change. Have fun you two."

"Thank you for making us beautiful, Laura," Katy said as Adam's sister left the room.

Jayne kept moving around the room, liking the way she looked. "Have you ever been to a wedding before Katy?"

"Yes. Quite a few."

"Have you ever caught the bouquet?"

"Twice. So don't believe that myth." Katy made a wry expression.

"Ah. Well. I don't think being married is something I want yet. I'm going to deal with my career first."

Katy chuckled. She liked Jayne.

•

Katy returned to her room to pick up her small purse and went downstairs. Adam was there in a black suit, crisp white shirt and black silk tie. He looked so handsome she felt her breath actually disappear for a few seconds.

The guests began to take their places around the poolside. Katy spotted Stella with a good-looking silver-haired man and Stella waved and smiled at her. Then, Katy's father, looking nervous, went to take his place by the pool to wait for his bride. Katy had never seen her father nervous, had never thought he was the agitated type. But he kept dragging on the cuffs of his white jacket and flicking imaginary lint from his dark pants.

"I hope he stops that fidgeting," Robert remarked to Katy before he walked past the waiting crowd to stand with his Dad.

She saw Robert talk to Paul and then she saw Robert begin to fidget like his father.

A few minutes later Trish, in a lemon silk suit, swished down the steps, Katy and Jayne behind her. All carried bouquets of yellow sweetheart roses and white daisies.

Katy saw real emotion in Paul Kerr's eyes for his new bride. When her father lifted the creamy veil and Trish's hand, with her glittering new rings, rested on her father's shoulder, she could tell their kiss was genuinely passionate and she felt tears prick her own eyes. She was pleased for her father. She hoped he would be happy.

Adam, standing beside her, handed her a white handkerchief. Gratefully, she carefully patted her eyes and smiled through a mist at him.

He leaned toward her ear. "I thought you weren't too excited about this union?"

"I'm not excited. I'm crying."

He chuckled and placed his hand on her waist to steady her.

Trish had the same people catering the meal as Adam had for his weekend. Somehow they managed to get everyone seated at tables set up throughout the rocky landscaping. A photographer moved through the guests, taking pictures.

After the dinner, a dance band set up.

Jayne said, "Dad arranged this. I'm going to talk to the guitarist."

Katy glanced to the guitarist who had curly black hair and a lean body in black gear. "He's very cute."

"Isn't he?" Jayne moved off and a while later Katy saw her talking to the musician.

They moved aside together and Katy noticed them talking to the keyboardist.

Jayne joined Katy again. "I told them I'm a singer. I don't really sing the type of stuff they play though."

"You were going to try and sing today?"

"I was going to show Dad."

"Not at your grandma's wedding, Jayne. Please."

The girl nodded. "Yeah, I guess you're right. It might spoil it."

"Your dad wouldn't be pleased and that would upset the wedding. Get me?"

"Yes, instead I'll go see if Greg will dance with me."

"I'm sure he will. Have fun."

"I will." Jayne swayed her hips. "Watch me."

Katy was pleased she'd diffused a possible situation as she observed Jayne talking to Greg. She turned away from where the dancing would be beside the pool to walk up the steps.

Her hand was grabbed. "Dance with me."

It was Adam, in the same vibrant mood he'd been in for the entire day. Sometimes Katy wondered if this mood was slightly forced, but she dismissed such thoughts as they began to dance to a set of slow tunes. She could feel the heat of his body through his suit jacket.

"I need to take off some clothes," he said and they walked away from the dancers. He shrugged out of his jacket and hung it on the branch of a tree. Then he loosened his tie.

"That'll do your jacket good," Katy said, striving for some normality. All she really wanted to do was melt into his body and dance some more.

He laughed and leaned over to kiss her and she wondered if anyone was watching.

When the bride and groom were on the verge of leaving, Trish tossed her bouquet into the crowd of unmarried women. The woman next to Katy caught it and Katy let out a huge sigh of relief. Not catching the bouquet eliminated all hope and expectations.

The newly married couple's departure became quite an event as they had loads of suitcases for their honeymoon. Jason, Paul, Robert and Adam had to keep repacking the trunk of her father's car until everything fit. Even then, the back seat was loaded. But eventually they drove off. Then one by one the guests, who weren't immediate family, left.

The silence was startling. All Katy could hear was the lap of water against rock, where Laura sat, stockings off, dangling her legs into the pool. Jason was in a tense, low-voiced conversation with Katy's brother about computers. Patty and the kids and had gone to bed. Jayne was in the house with Greg, who had driven his parents' to their hotel. Which left Adam and Katy. She had thought, after the intimacy of the dancing they might stay together, but instead, he went up to the house.

Feeling ignored and let down, a condition she knew was unreasonable, Katy said goodnight and went to the house herself. She found Adam, Jayne and Greg in the kitchen doing a cleaning job.

Dismissing the letdown feeling as being stupidly selfish, Katy asked if she could help.

"We're managing," Jayne told her. The girl was now dressed in jeans and T-shirt, as was Greg.

"There's not too much left to do," Adam said. "It's just that we're the ones who have to close down the house tomorrow. And we will take the cats home with us."

"You're taking the cats to your place?"

"Yep," Jayne said. "Your dad and grandma are planning on lots of travels. We're going to keep them."

"For good?"

"Yes." Jayne seemed excited about the two cats staying.

By the time the others found the nighttime bugs too annoying and the breeze from the lake cold, the kitchen was spotless.

"Successful day," Jason said.

"Successful day," Adam echoed. "And I'm bushed."

As Jayne was still around, Katy said her goodnights and went up to the blue room. One more day to go, she thought as she prepared for bed. Despite the good times they'd had together this weekend, she was under no illusions. She knew she might only see Adam on rare occasions in the future.

•

Adam went for his last morning walk of the weekend. He could have stayed here for a week, maybe longer. He would like to stay here alone with Katy so they could be together. They needed to be together if they were ever going to nurture a relationship. But all he had was today and tomorrow, and then he was gone again until Thursday.

He returned to the house, showered and dressed, then found Jayne in the kitchen talking on her cell phone. When she disconnected, she said sweetly, "Dad?"

"What?" He poured himself coffee.

"Greg and his parents want to drive me home. We'll take the cats."

"Greg's parents don't mind taking the cats?"

"No. They don't mind. Then you don't have to worry and I can go home with Greg. I have to call him back to let him know. They're coming by to pick me up in an hour."

"Well." It meant he would be alone with Katy. "Okay. Go get the cats in their carriers and I'll bring your luggage down."

"Thanks." She began punching numbers on the phone.

Adam drained his coffee and went upstairs to get Jayne's bags, which were neatly packed by the door. He figured she knew last night she might be going with Greg. Why else was she up so early?

By the time he put Jayne's luggage by the front door Katy was up dressed in black Capri pants and a white T-shirt.

"Jayne said she's going with Greg," Katy said.

"Yes. They're taking the cats as well, so we won't have to worry about that."

He was annoyed the weekend was quickly sneaking to an end and he felt as if he had lost control again. "We'll leave after everyone else has gone."

•

Adam seemed a trifle cool this morning. Or was it that his effervescent mood from the rest of the weekend had evaporated? Whatever it was, he wasn't quite the same. He didn't give Katy any warm lingering looks or touch her unnecessarily. Maybe he'd been nice to her because of the wedding and now the wedding was over he wanted to get rid of her.

Robert and Patty left before them. Beside the minivan, Robert said to Katy, "Behave," giving her a look that told her he was reminding her of the incident in the kitchen.

She grinned. "I wouldn't worry. He's a workaholic."

Rob laughed. "Okay, but don't dismiss him. He seems to be a nice guy. The boys are crazy about him. He let them keep those fishing rods and all the tackle."

"That's great, Rob."

"Yeah. Trish has invited us here anytime we want to come. She's going to live with Dad in the condo, but they'll keep this house as well. She has a couple who can live in."

"Seems like everything is arranged then. You'll probably see more of Dad now that he has a new wife."

"We want to see you as well, Katy. Patty and I have been thinking of taking a break from the boys. We thought we would stay in Toronto for a weekend on one of those hotel specials."

"That would be wonderful," Katy told him, meaning it. She really did want to keep her family together.

"Then we'll let you know ahead of time."

"Great." Katy saw Patty piling the kids into the van. "Have a safe journey home."

"You too."

After hugs and kisses, Katy waved the van goodbye.

Not much later Jason's Lexus pulled out of the driveway. Adam suggested he pack their luggage in his car, so Katy went to get her clothes together. She packed, checked the room, and went downstairs.

The drive home was on the freeway, with one stop for coffee and a snack. Being the weekend, parking was at a premium on her street. Adam carried her bags for her. She had the feeling that this was it. No more family get-togethers were planned. Her stomach felt hollow with the promise of the end.

When she opened the front door the apartment was stuffy. Adam put down her luggage. "It's stifling in here. Don't you have air conditioning?"

"There's one in the window in the second bedroom, but it doesn't work very well."

He sighed. "You know, if you want, you can ditch this place and come and stay at my house for the summer, until you have somewhere."

Katy looked at him. "Why?"

"Well, Jayne's there, and you could use the studio, work up for your audition."

"You want me to take over your responsibility for Jayne for the summer?"

"Okay, yes. It would help to have you there."

"I don't know, Adam. Let me think about it." She wasn't sure that she wanted to live that close to Adam, even if he wasn't around most of the time. She walked to the window but the window wouldn't budge.

"I'll open the windows for you. They look old and sticky." Adam moved in front of her and lifted each sash window easily and pulled back the blinds. The weather was a lot cooler than it had been on Thursday and a soft breeze blew through.

"That's better. Thank you."

"Do you want to go out for something to eat?" Adam asked.

"Not really. Why don't I cook you something here?"

"Sounds good."

"Spaghetti and beer?"

"I'd love a beer. And spaghetti sounds fantastic."

While he poured beer into two glasses, Adam watched Katy mix some spaghetti sauce. He hadn't been in a domestic situation with a woman for so long or maybe never that Adam enjoyed sharing a meal with her. For a while eating with her in the small kitchen and helping with the dishes afterwards, he felt quite normal, quite relaxed. Their kiss before he left was satisfying enough to let him think he had a chance with her.

There was a car in the driveway when he arrived home. He knew it was the Carson's family vehicle. He let himself into a house now full of cats and Jayne's luggage in the foyer. He wasn't surprised to find his daughter and Greg in an embrace in the living room.

He cleared his throat at the door and the couple jumped apart.

"Dad." Jayne touched her mouth. "Where've you been?"

He jangled his keys. "I took Katy home and had dinner with her."

Adam glanced at Greg who was sort of hovering in the shadows. "Don't you think it's late, Greg?"

"We were just saying goodnight," Greg told him. "I'll see you, Jayne."

"I'll see you out," Jayne said and gave Adam a glare as she passed him at the door.

Monster rubbed at his ankles and Adam hunkered down to pat him. "I'm a fine one to talk? Is that what you're telling me? Because I think I've fallen in love myself."

He saw to Jayne's luggage and went downstairs again as she came in.

"Dad. Will you please not be rude to Greg."

"I didn't think I was exactly rude."

"You act as if he's doing something wrong. I wanted that kiss. We had a good weekend together."

"That's fine. As long as it's only a kiss."

His daughter stuck her hands insolently into the back pockets of her jeans. "It's okay for you to have girlfriends. I'm presuming Katy is a girlfriend. But it's not okay for me to have boyfriends. Right? It's okay for everyone else to have a music career, but not okay for me. Right?"

Adam shook his head. He didn't really know what to say. He was losing his little girl and gaining a woman who fought on the same ground he did. "Okay, we'll let it go. Greg's a nice guy, just be careful, and we'll discuss the music, okay?"

She grinned. "I'll accept the music, but I'm not going that far with Greg."

Relief swamped him. "You don't like him that much then?"

"He's okay. He's also got a super job lined up in Boston for September, so he'll be gone from my turf. I'm not going to get myself all worked up over a guy who's not going to be here."

*Which could be Katy's song,* Adam thought as he locked up the house later. He didn't know how he was going to work a relationship with her, but in the meantime he had to train his mind back to business. Tomorrow, New York.

# Chapter Fourteen

It was a humid, cloudy day with thunder rumbling in the distance when Katy made her way home from the restaurant. She hadn't been working as a waitress, but behind the scenes on the accounts. They were showing a substantial profit so she felt pleased about the venture. Still, she didn't like spending all her savings on the rent for this apartment. Maybe she should go and live at Adam's house and work at his studio. He was never home anyway.

After a shower, she put on her denim shorts and a white cotton halter and poured herself a tall glass of lemonade. Holding the glass, she walked to the window to open the blind more fully so she would be able to see to play the piano. The day was turning really dark. She had heard something on the radio about a storm.

Meeting Adam hadn't really put her in a good place emotionally, but he'd promised her an audition, and she needed to work something up to show him. She glanced at the piano. She was almost frightened to go and sit down and play. It was like her confidence had left her.

Instead, she sat at her laptop and put in a search for Adam's name as she'd promised herself to do a long time ago. She'd had to connect her own computer to the internet since Joe moved out his stuff.

There wasn't much about him, other than a web page for SMM. She tried a search for Rachel Frank. There were old videos from performances and a couple of biographies, but nothing about her connection to Adam. He'd kept himself very private.

An impatient, honking car horn made her look outside again. A limousine blocked the street between the two lines of parked cars. Adam leaned in the window talking to the driver. When he finished talking, he saluted the line of cars behind the limo and came to Katy's front door. She saw the limo move off and went to open the door. Adam was completely unexpected and she wasn't sure if she felt glad, or sad, that he would just arrive here with no previous notification. It was as if he expected her to be waiting for him.

He wore a light gray suit, white shirt and a silver tie, looking tall and handsome and wonderful. She had missed him terribly and she wished she hadn't.

He echoed her feelings. "I've missed you, Katy." He took her into his arms. "Hell, I've missed you."

She avoided wrapping her arms around him. "When did you get back?"

"I had Todd drive me straight here from the airport. I haven't been to the office yet. So I have three hours before a four-thirty meeting."

Katy knew what he'd come for. The reason was the rigid hard-on, the trembling kiss he placed on her mouth, the way his palms stroked her back. She pushed him away.

"What do you want to drink?"

"What's the matter?" He followed her into the kitchen.

She poured another glass of lemonade. "I'm annoyed because the writing is on the wall; I'm going to become a slot in your diary. I've been through this routine before, Adam, and I'm not going through it again." She handed the glass to him.

"What if I tell you it's not going to be just the three hours today, Katy. I want to invite you to my place for the weekend. Jayne is going to stay with Molly. And Stella isn't back until Monday. We'll have a lot of time together. We can discuss you coming to stay for the summer."

"Even if I'm at your house you're hardly there."

He stood the glass on the table and came around to stand in front of her. He pried her glass from her fingers. "I have to do my job. You have to do yours as well. You'll be able to do that at the house. We need to make love, to confirm that we're a couple. I'm burning up for you, woman."

She was in his arms again and she couldn't resist him. He stroked her hair, kissed her neck, her ears, her mouth, He whispered. "You smell so sweet."

"Body wash," she said.

And he laughed. "You always have to drop in the reality."

"Reality is a problem with me." Then because she couldn't help it, she hugged him. "But I've missed you as well, Adam."

"At least I know when you say something, you mean it. Do you want me?"

She did. But where would it lead her?

"Then we've got three hours. Look, Katy, if you pursue your music to the hilt, you'll be in the same situation, giving me ultimatums for time. I know, I've seen it."

She sighed. He was right. She really couldn't turn down a relationship with a man she knew she was in love with because of a future she had no control over.

He stepped away from her. "Bedroom. Slow and easy. I love you, Katy."

She was pleased she had stopped for a moment to tidy her room this morning. It was small but it looked inviting with the black cushions on the dusky pink quilt. The furniture was sparse but good leftovers from her parents' house.

"It's very nice," he said.

Adam closed the door and loosened his tie. He undid the top buttons on his shirt. Then his gaze took in all of her from her bare silver painted toenails to the tiny halter covering her breasts. He stopped at her eyes and kept his gaze there. She realized she was hot and trembling inside and she knew he was well aware of his effect on her. She didn't want anything else this afternoon but to make love with Adam.

He slipped out of his jacket and tossed it on to an armchair then he walked over to her. He lifted the halter over her head and glanced down at her breasts. He pressed his mouth to the gentle swell and let his tongue moisten each nipple. Katy closed her eyes and brought her hands up to hold his head. How long ago had she seen his hair against his collar and wanted him?

Katy fumbled with his shirt buttons until they were undone, then she stroked her palms over his chest and leaned down to kiss his smooth golden muscles. She heard his breath catch and her hand found its way to his belt.

"Undo it."

She slipped the buckle on his belt and slid her hand down to touch him. She heard him groan and she met his gaze and saw his eyes were full of dark passion. Their lips met again and the kiss that flared was full of hunger and urgency taking them naked to the bed.

For a brief second there was a hesitation, then Adam was sliding inside her and Katy knew that whatever happened this was the man she was going to love forever.

She was beautiful, soft and willing. Her legs came around him, easing him inside her until he was on the point of explosion. When she threw back her head and began to cry out, Adam let all of his emotions go with the sensations that flooded him. All of his worries and fears, everything he had stored for years, disappeared. The heat of the moment was a brilliant rush, until all he could feel was the pumping of his heart and Katy's shallow breathing beneath him. He kissed her mouth and she kissed him lightly back.

"I don't want to leave you," he said and he meant it.

She entwined her arms around his neck. "Don't leave me then."

"We have a while."

"Yes." Her body wriggled beneath him and her breathing grew rapid again.

And so did his when he ran his hands down her deliciously curvy body. This time he thought he could take it slower but she stirred his fire and made him burn. In no time they were in a desperate struggle together for another blinding flash of pleasure.

When they parted, finally, Katy slid off the bed. "I'll get our drinks."

Adam lay against the pillow unable to take his eyes off her creamy limbs. He heard a distant rumble of thunder and he felt a rare security of being here with Katy in bed. As if whatever happened they were together.

She brought in their glasses plus a package of chocolate chip cookies.

"Good diet," Adam said, sitting up against the pillows, while she snuggled beside him.

He wondered if Joe had ever been in this room, if he'd sat in her bed and been treated to chocolate chip cookies and lemonade. He couldn't bear it if he was only one of many, the way he had discovered he had been with Rachel. Then he became angry with himself. *Don't jeopardize this opportunity,* Stevenson.

"They're great cookies," she said, looking at him as if she could sense his fear.

He bit into one. "They are." Then, surprising himself, he laughed out loud because it was happiness he suddenly felt, not fear.

"What's up?" she asked.

"Not used to me laughing?"

She stroked his chest. "Not in quite such a spontaneous way."

"Call it spontaneous combustion caused by Katy Kerr." He kissed her nose. "Will you come to my place for the weekend?"

"Probably now I will."

"Great. I'll have Todd pick you up in the limo and bring you to SMM. Then we'll drive from there in my car."

"We would be starting something for sure, Adam."

"We've already started something."

"True." Then she smiled. "But I've never been in a

limo. That would be neat."

He was pleased to make her happy. "We have forty minutes left," he said, easing her on top of his body, so he could gaze at her breasts and the slope of her stomach to the delicious dark triangle. She kissed his nose, his mouth and he let her have full control over him. Once more to last him until Friday.

•

The limo blocked the road right on four. Adam tied his tie in the back seat and raked his fingers through hair still damp from Katy's shower. His body wasn't sated. It still desired. He couldn't wait for the weekend. He grinned foolishly to himself and he saw Todd raise an eyebrow.

"I want you to pick up Ms. Kerr on Friday afternoon at five o'clock, Todd and bring her to my office. I'll have my car to go home in."

"Great, Adam," Todd said. "It's about time you got serious with someone. Even if she does live on a street that's a tight fit for this vehicle."

Adam scratched his jaw. "Yeah. Her dad just married my mother the other week."

"That's where she comes from," Todd said, light dawning. "That's wonderful. Two weddings and a— what was the name of that old movie?"

"I believe it was four and a funeral. But we'll leave off the latter. It's the last thing we need. And don't rush another wedding either. She might not want me."

Todd, who had been married for fifteen years with two children, considered marriage the only way to live. "It seemed like she wanted you this afternoon."

"Yes." Adam agreed but self-doubt lurked. He'd fallen in love before, granted not like this, but he'd never been able to nurture the relationships. This time he was going to have to make some changes to keep her.

He saw an ominous flash of lightning and looked out of the window. Rain pounded the asphalt and the day had turned extremely dull. His cheer after being with Katy diminished, as if he had been in a sunny place, and now was shrouded in darkness. Thunder still rumbled when Adam entered SMM and gave him a bad case of depression.

Alison was working hard at her computer. She stopped when she saw him.

"Hi. Where've you been? Ty has been calling wanting to talk to you. We thought you would be here by now. Your plane got in from New York ages ago."

"I had some things to take care of."

"Great. But you know Ty. He wants everyone jumping yesterday. He's scouting songs for Lilah's new CD he's producing. They figure she needs something more upbeat to bring her up-to-date. He wants to know if you've come across any really startling musicians lately that Lilah could work with."

"Okay. Thanks, Alison."

Adam walked into his office and took off his jacket. He tossed it over the back of his chair. His desk was piled high with messages but he ignored them thinking about Katy. Could she collaborate with Lilah? It might give Lilah a boost and ease Katy into the limelight. He just didn't know how good a song writer and singer Katy really was yet.

He sat back in his chair, his arms folded. He remembered all the bad, really bad, music and performers he had listened to over the years. But he also remembered the not-quite-there but good, the gems that needed polishing, and the forceful talent like Jayne's mother that couldn't be stopped. Stars in the making. He remembered listening to Katy play the piano. There'd been something raw that he'd liked.

This weekend, he'd get Katy into his studio and he would look at Katy's work with objectivity. He would forget about hurting her. He would be professional and tell her the truth. It might be brutal but that's how this business ran. In his experience, if an artist was really good, brutality would only reinforce their desire to succeed.

The buzzer went. His appointment was here.

•

Katy shoved the last of her things into her weekend bag and slipped on a black cotton jacket over her jeans and white cotton top. The limousine was blocking the road.

On the street Todd held the limousine door open and Katy slid into the back seat. While he put her luggage into the trunk, she made herself comfortable. There was another long seat facing her and two small ones that pulled down. In the middle was a phone, a bar, a monitor or TV, a music player with some computer equipment attached and lots of other buttons. From behind the tinted windows, Katy felt as if she were divided from the world. She wasn't sure if she enjoyed the feeling very much, she was such a down-on-the-streets-with-the-people type of person. She wondered if that was why Adam drove his own car most of the time. He didn't take advantage of his wealth and position to put him into a bubble.

The trip out to the industrial park didn't seem to take long. As Todd edged the long car through the parking lot and she saw Adam's car parked at the back of the building, Katy felt her heart beat faster. She had gone further with Adam than she'd ever intended and she was truly in love with him.

Todd told her he would transfer her luggage to Adam's car and he showed her through the back door and along a corridor to a pair of wooden double doors.

"This is Adam's suite. He said, if he's not here, to make yourself comfortable."

Katy smiled. "Thank you, Todd."

Todd left her alone and she pushed open one of the doors. Adam's suite was right. It was the entire corner of the building. There was another door, partly open, leading from the large outer office that had enough comfortable chairs to furnish a couple of living rooms. The colors were the SMM colors: silver and black. A woman with long, dark hair wearing jeans and a T-shirt was kneeling on the floor pulling stuck pages from the photocopying machine.

When she heard the door close, she looked up. "Sorry. Are you, Katy?"

"Yes. I am."

"I'm Alison Fortune. I don't usually crawl around the floor, but this machine has been playing up all day." Alison rose to her feet and came over to shake Katy's hand. "Adam will be back in a few seconds. He's just having a last minute meeting with Ty and Rory."

As if Katy knew who those people were. Rory, she presumed was Rory Dean. Was she going to meet him?

"Finish what you're doing," Katy told Alison. "I'll wait."

"Do you want to wait in Adam's office? I'll get you something to drink if you like. Pop, coffee?"

"I'm fine. But I will wait in Adam' office."

Alison opened the other door. The windows were covered by vertical blinds letting in a shadowed light to fall over the rich oak furniture and black and chrome leather sofa and chairs.

"Thank you," she told Alison.

Alison closed the door on her and Katy stood for a moment getting her bearings. Adam's office was spacious, just like his house. Hanging from the walls were all sorts of music memorabilia. A brass tag mentioned a certain guitar had belonged to Rachel Frank, Jayne's mother. There were also photographs of stars like Rory accepting platinum disks and a huge portrait of Lilah Payne when she was younger.

Katy decided to sit down on a chair close to Adam's desk. As soon as she was seated, Alison popped her head in the door.

"Hi. The photocopier is fixed now and the panic is over. I'm leaving. I have to pick up my little boy as his father is away. Adam called up. He'll be five at most."

"Fine," Katy said. "Have a good weekend."

"You too, Katy." Alison grinned. "See you again."

*They all know why I'm here,* Katy thought, as she crossed her legs and looked at her white sandals, noticing a scuff mark on one of the straps crossing her foot. She should have worn black.

She glanced around the office, feeling as if her eyes were a camera scanning the shot. She didn't feel comfortable. She wasn't cut out to be a rich man's play thing. She wanted to pursue her music career, granted, but she only wanted the work, not the trimmings. If she ever became famous, people would say she'd slept with Adam Stevenson and that was the only reason she was successful. She could leave now, she supposed. It wouldn't take much to call a cab and meet it out on the road. Nothing would be lost. She might never see Adam again. But that was what could happen anyway. He could easily get tired of her in a weekend. Now she wished she had accepted a pop from Alison because her throat felt like a sand quarry.

The door flung open and Adam strode in. He wore jeans and a lightweight black sweatshirt. He was followed by two men. One was Rory Dean, who was a tall, slim man, showing his age a bit in his crinkled tanned features. Rory's pale hair was short and he wore a silver earring, jeans and a T-shirt. The other man was stout in a suit and had wild, dark blonde hair.

"Katy," Adam said as Katy jumped to her feet. "This is Rory Dean. Ty Holden. Katy Kerr."

She shook hands with Rory Dean and he smiled at her and said, "Hi, Katy. How's it going?"

"Fine. Thank you." She tried not to look as if she were in awe. *Cool, Katy. Cool.*

Ty pumped her hand as well and she remembered who he was. She'd seen his name on the credits of many a CD. He was an internationally sought-after producer. He wasn't a startling good looking man but his features were rugged enough to be interesting. He looked as if he had been around in every way.

He said, "Katy. Pleased to meet you."

Rory said, "Anyway, Adam, I'm leaving. Talk to you in a few days time."

"I'll grab a lift with you," Ty told him. "See you Adam. Katy."

Rory glanced back. "Good to meet you, Katy."

The doors flapped shut.

Adam perched on the edge of his desk. "So how are you today?"

She swept her arm around his office. "A little in awe of all this."

He smiled. "Don't be. I'm just a man who has built up a good living."

"Oh, yeah."

He came over to her and kissed her mouth. "Let's go home."

Katy felt Adam's hand on her waist as they went down the corridor and out of the back door. She slipped into the BMW beside him. At least the car felt familiar, as did the sight of Adam's strong hands on the steering wheel. Had she actually lain naked beneath this man, made love with him? She remembered the way he had allowed her to make love to him. She'd kissed him all over his body. She'd touched him with her hands she'd writhed and twisted until she blew his mind. She felt as if she should've been more cautious with him. He held more of her future in his hands than she'd ever let any man.

"Something the matter?" Adam asked her.

"Why?"

"You seem very tense."

"I am tense," she said honestly. "I'm not used to being picked up by a limousine and meeting famous people. I'm not used to you really."

Silently he reached over and took hold of her fingers. He didn't let go until the car stopped outside his house. Inside, they were greeted by the patter of paws and tiny meows from the cats.

"How are they doing?" Katy asked as Adam carried her luggage upstairs and she followed.

"Great. They like it here. Jayne spoils them rotten."

"That's good." She went with him into the oak and burgundy bedroom. "Everywhere you live there is so much space."

Adam put her bag near the closet. "You don't like space?"

"I love space. But I'm used to small and cluttered. At least I have been since I left home."

"That's what I'm thinking. You told me your mother liked neat and tidy."

"She did. We had a big two-story four bedroom house."

"Well, then." He smiled. "But we can move into a smaller room for the weekend if you want to."

"No. It's fine." She thought he looked so handsome in his jeans, jacket and sweatshirt, with his thick brown hair slightly ruffled from the breeze outside and his jaw shadowed. So handsome her insides ached. She didn't want to ache when she was with Adam. She wanted to enjoy her blossoming love.

She glanced around the bedroom. She was going to be here in this bed with him for a couple of nights. She wasn't sure she was really ready for this, but she was here now, in the middle of a dream.

# Chapter Fifteen

Katy awoke on Sunday morning to the sound of the birds and the bright hot sunshine of a warm day. Inside her stomach was a sinking sensation that the hours with Adam were dwindling. She buried her face into her pillow. The weekend had been wonderful. Lovemaking by the pool at midnight with the moon shining through the glass dome—on Adam's bed in the sunrise. Katy reached across the bed and touched Adam's cool pillow. It seemed he had been gone from the bed for some time.

She slid out of the bed, showered and dressed in her black shorts and a white top. Despite the air-conditioning being turned on in the house, her flesh felt sticky as she walked down the stairs. In the kitchen she found coffee had been made. The cats had been fed and lay preening themselves on a rug in the sunshine.

She heard Adam's voice and discovered him in his study. The door was wide open and Adam, wearing cargo shorts and a loose shirt, was speaking on his phone. He paced the soft carpet against the light wood-paneled walls.

Adam saw her and saluted to her. Katy half-heartedly waved back. He kept talking. "Let's put it this way—"

Was he the same as her former boyfriend? Except this time when the relationship ended she would feel much worse. This time she was so much in love she felt physically and spiritually connected to Adam. She turned away from his study and returned to the kitchen, where she poured herself some coffee into a mug and sat looking absently out of the window at the patio. Jinx and Monster rubbed around her ankles and she nuzzled their fur with her bare toes. When Adam came in, she looked at him.

"Sorry," he said, pouring his own coffee.

"It's okay." But it wasn't. She heard a sob in the back of her voice.

He perched beside her on the next stool. "Rory wants to quit the business."

"That's understandable."

"Why would you say that?"

Katy felt him lift a lock of hair and kiss her neck. She said shakily, "Because it's a career that is so demanding on a personal life."

"That's the truth. So are you having second thoughts about your own career?"

"No. I'm not talking about myself. All I've done is play a few gigs, go home and on the street the next day no one knows who I am."

"Do you want to be famous?"

"I'm not sure. I really don't think my strength is in my performing. I was told once by an agent that I should concentrate on the song writing."

He sat up on a stool next to her. "Well, that might be true. Why don't we go into the studio? I'm thinking that we could promote you a different way. Do you know Lilah Payne's work?"

"Of course. I love her."

"And a lot of people do, but we can't book her into large venues these days. She needs a new sound. She's not been writing much herself either. Katy if your songs suit her you could collaborate with Lilah on her next record."

Katy stared at him. "You want me to work with Lilah Payne?"

"Yes. You could even sing with her. Lilah's voice is quite sweet. Maybe a duet might be in order, and add strength to the overall sound. You know, featuring Katy Kerr. It would ease you into the biz. You possibly might be a better song writer than performer. Have you written many songs?"

"Loads," Katy told him, not quite believing what he was saying. To work with Lilah Payne would be a dream come true.

"Come on, bring your coffee. Let's go to the studio."

For the remainder of the morning Katy dug into the depths of her mind for songs she'd composed. She was amazed she remembered most of them. She sang, she played the piano, she performed for Adam. He sat silently watching her, listening. She would've thought he'd be restless but he wasn't. He was patient when it came to assessing performers and music.

"Okay," he said at last. "You're amazing. Really you are. You're certainly a born songwriter, a poet. Lilah will love your work."

"You think?"

"I know, Katy. She's looking for new songs. She writes a few but they do tend to stick into a slow tempo groove. A few upbeat tunes and she could be on the charts again. Then if they're good and we see a chance, you could tour with her."

Katy shook her head. "I can't believe you're saying this."

"You're attractive and you're emotionally involved with your songs and music. You're good, really good."

"You're not just saying that because we're lovers?"

"No way. Although I do think that you are more of a composer than a singer. You've got a nice voice. Have you ever had any training?"

"No. I learned to play the piano when I was a child and it enabled me to write songs. When Joe came into Heather's life, he suggested I get some gigs. He introduced me to his agent."

"Joe?"

"I told you before that he has a band."

"Right." Adam rose to his feet. "Okay, we'll wind up now and have some lunch, and I'll get back to you about Lilah."

Katy didn't want to get too excited. What if Lilah thought it was a bad idea to have an unknown artist work with her? So she kept her thoughts calm as she swam with Adam in the pool and read a book while he was busy in his office. They had a light dinner and Katy went up to the room to pack.

Minutes from now she would be leaving this house. Tomorrow Adam was going to California until Wednesday. Would he want her when he returned on Wednesday? And where was he going after that?

This was silly. She'd just experienced one of the best weekends of her life, she had an opening for her career, and she was making herself miserable by creating a horror of a future. But she couldn't stop the ache.

"Katy? Let's go."

Katy rose from the bed and Adam lifted her bag and carried it downstairs to the car. All the way home, she wondered when and if she would see him again.

He parked the car as close to her apartment as possible and helped her with her luggage.

"I'll give you a call on Wednesday," he said after a kiss. "All right?"

"All right," Katy told him.

He tipped her chin with his finger. "Don't look so down. We had a great weekend."

"We did."

"But you have something on your mind."

"Nothing that can't wait," she said and gave him an extra kiss on his cheek. "Take care."

"You too."

"You know," he said. "If you leave your cell phone on I'll send you a text."

"Okay. I'll do that."

Katy watched the car take off feeling as if part of her had just left with Adam.

•

Jayne wasn't yet home as Adam opened the door to a quiet house. He missed Katy already. But he also began to worry about Jayne. She had driven her own car to Rory's farm North of Toronto to spend the weekend with Molly and she had quite a long highway trip home.

He knew of course she wouldn't want to leave too early after having spent most of their time in Rory's new studio, a studio Adam still had to visit. Rory told him he was planning a family and friends get together soon.

Impatient for Jayne to come home, Adam began tidying up the house that had become a trifle messy. But he felt good about the weekend. He'd enjoyed every moment.

He'd been relieved that Katy's music had been more than good, excellent, and that he was able to tell her the truth.

Adam had just finished making the bed in the room by the pool, where he'd last made love with Katy, when he heard his daughter's car drive into the garage. Relief shrouded him and he went to let Jayne in through the mud room door before the alarm went off.

Jayne looked tanned and healthy in her white shorts and denim shirt. Her long, silky hair flowed around her shoulders, and he thought he saw some highlights in her hair and wondered if they were real from the sun or injected by Molly who loved to fiddle around with hair color. He carried her overnight bag for her. "Did you have a good time?"

She dragged her backpack with her. "Fan-tas-tic. Two musicians from that group from the wedding came over. Molly's dating the drummer."

*Great.* They entered the annex hallway. "Who were you with?"

"Liam the guitarist. He's cool."

*Double great.*

"The new studio is so cool. Dad, you should see it, well, you will. Uncle Rory's inviting us all out next weekend."

"I guess you spent most of the weekend in the studio," Adam said casually.

"Yep." She looked very perky, as if she'd got her way with him and won the battle. "Ty came in for a while and he said he was going to talk to you about me and a recording label."

"He did, did he?"

"I'm going ahead with it, Dad. I'll negotiate my own deals if you won't help me, or I'll go to someone else. Or maybe I'll even go to New York or L.A."

She was yanking on the chain and he could feel it like a noose about his throat. "All right. Later."

"Don't keep saying later. Later is too late. I have to do this now, even before I finish university."

"What am I supposed to say?"

"Go ahead kid. I'll help you. Rory helps Molly."

"I'll think about it.

"Wow," Jayne said. "You're doing well. We've moved up a notch, from later to think about it. So what did you do here all alone?"

He debated whether he should tell her or not, but then thought about how serious he felt about Katy. He wanted to pave the way in case he might want to get married. So he cleared his throat and stated, "I wasn't alone. Katy was here."

They had reached the downstairs foyer. Jayne dumped her backpack by the palm plant. She made a face at her father. "I thought you were over her."

"No. I'm not over her. I'm just getting warmed up with her."

Her eyes grew wide. "You mean you did stuff with her. Here in this house?"

He put down her bag. "It's my house. I care about her. I'm not going to sneak around with her."

She squeezed her eyes shut to stop the tears. "Oh, Dad." Then she slapped her forehead with the palm of her hand. "I can't believe this is happening."

"Why not?" he asked. "Isn't it about time? I need someone."

She circled the foyer in front of him.

"Jayne. Think of it this way. You're already starting to do your own thing without me."

"Yes. But it's always just been you and me."

"I know that. But already you have boyfriends and you'll go away and I— Dammit, I'm still young."

"Are you going to marry her?"

He told the truth. "Possibly."

"So she'll come here to live?"

"Of course."

She stopped wandering around. "Yikes."

He chuckled. "What does that mean, exactly?"

"I never thought about you getting married."

"Well, start thinking about it because it might happen."

She gave him a narrow eyed look. "It might also happen that I become a singer. I'll live with you getting married, if you can live with that."

He matched her narrow look. "That's not fair."

"Yes. It is. Anyway, you're lucky because I like Katy. I do think she'll be good for you." She came over and hugged him. "I'm pleased for you, Dad. Really I am."

He gave her a return hug. "Let's be happy," he said.

"Yep," she said then picked up her backpack. "I'd really like something to eat."

"I'll fix some sandwiches. See you in the kitchen."

Adam walked into the kitchen and pulled out some of the fixings from the fridge. Maybe with Katy and Jayne he'd have a chance at more of a family life in his future.

•

He did say Wednesday, didn't he?

The sun was dipping over the city buildings and he

hadn't called. No text either and Katy had left her cell phone on, assiduously charging the battery every night. She'd even composed a new song, *Useless Words*. She sat at the piano penning lyrics on to a sheet of paper.

*Text him?*

*No.*

*Why not?*

*I don't want to seem as if I'm chasing him.*

Her cell phone suddenly pealed out the song she'd put on as a ring tone. She saw Adam's name. Her heart thudded as she answered it. "Hello."

"Hello to you," Adam said with a chuckle.

Relief flooded her body. "Where have you been? You said Wednesday."

"The plane was delayed. If it's okay I'm on my way over."

"You're calling from your car?"

"That's right. See you in about fifteen minutes."

Quickly, Katy changed into a pair of white cotton pants and a cool lace blouse. She dragged a brush through her hair until it looked casual and bouncy. Then she put on fresh make-up. The doorbell rang before she chose any shoes, so she ran barefoot to answer the door.

Adam closed the door and swung her into his arms. Their kiss lasted for ages and when they drew apart they were both breathing hard.

"I have missed you," he said in husky tones.

"I missed you too."

He grinned. "I can tell. So let's get busy."

It was heaven to be held by Adam once more, to feel his naked body entwining with hers, to cry out her pleasure with him.

He said, stroking her hair. "I want to wake up with you every morning, Katy. I can't bear being apart from you. Marry me? I really think we'll have a good life together."

She wasn't sure. "I don't know, Adam. You're away so much."

"You'll be busy. I still have to talk to Lilah, but I'm sure that deal will work out."

Katy touched his brow. "That is not the reason I would marry you. In fact, it's another reason I wouldn't marry you."

"Okay. So marry me for crazy reasons, like we can't stay away from one another." Adam moved over her body.

"Marry you for sex?" she asked, taking him into her. He nibbled her ear. "Yes. Marry me for sex."

"Only if you love me," she whispered.

"I love you," he said softly into her ear, beginning a slow thrusting movement. "I love you."

•

Katy sat back in the comfortable limousine to go to Adam's house on Saturday morning. From Adam's, they would travel to Rory Dean's home for the weekend. And she'd agreed to marry him, even if she felt uneasy about the decision. When the limousine pulled up in front of Adam's house, he came outside to greet her. Holding her hand, he led her through the door. Jayne came down the stairs wearing jeans and a T-shirt and carrying a bag.

"Hi, Katy," Jayne said.

"Hi," Katy replied. Adam had told her that Jayne was okay about their relationship but she sensed a wariness coming from Adam's daughter. She understood completely where Jayne was coming from and she didn't want to antagonize her. "Looking forward to the week-end?"

"Yes. Are you?"

"Yes. I am."

Adam's fingers squeezed hers. "Jayne," Adam said. "Go put your stuff in the car. We have to be there for lunch."

"Who's going to be there?" Katy asked.

"Rory, Carolyn, Molly, Lilah and her husband, Bill. It's sort of a studio launch. Rory's in a conundrum. One part of his brain wants to keep a studio going for his performing. The other wants to retire and raise goats."

"Musical goats?" she said with a smile.

Adam grinned. "No. Real goats. Milk, cheese, baby goats. Because of this, I've been playing therapist for the past six months."

"I never thought of you as a therapist."

"Well, I am. Sometimes." He leaned over and kissed her. "Anyway, I have something for you." He opened her hand, slipped his hand into his pocket and pressed a ring into her palm. "If you don't like it, tell me honestly."

The diamonds formed the shape of a flower. "Adam," was all Katy could say.

"I hope you like it?" He placed his hands in the air. "I know men aren't supposed to do this type of thing these days. You would prefer to choose your own ring. Is that it?"

She should tell him she was strictly in this for love, not the treats, but she didn't want to upset him. "Of course I like it. It's beautiful." She held the gorgeous ring up to him. "Put it on my finger."

He slid it on her finger. Then he kissed the ring and

her finger. "Now our engagement is official."

She was officially going to Rory Dean's as Adam's fiancée. Even so, Katy still felt trepidation as she showed Jayne her ring before they climbed into the car.

"It's really pretty," Jayne said, surprising Katy with her warmth. "Congratulations."

At least Jayne's acceptance of the engagement made the drive to Rory's bearable and the three of them talked amongst themselves as Adam drove them through rolling green countryside. When he turned off the highway he followed a smaller winding road darkened and cooled by overhanging trees. At a red mailbox they followed a driveway to a house. It was a well hidden property. To one side of the upright stone house was a cultivated garden and across a grass field was another stone building that looked new enough to be the studio.

A woman wearing jeans and a check shirt came out of the house to greet them. She was pretty, with long dark hair and a ready smile. Adam introduced Katy to Carolyn Dean.

Carolyn said warmly, "So pleased to meet you. Rory mentioned that Adam had met someone. We're so thrilled. Hi, Jayne. And Adam. Congratulations." They were all treated to hugs. "Come on into the house and I'll get Mike to bring in your things." Carolyn glanced at Katy. "Mike's our son."

Adam's warm hand was on Katy's waist as Carolyn led them through the front door into a cool hallway. The floors were highly polished wood and the furniture was sparse but beautiful. They went out to a huge kitchen, adjoined by an atrium furnished with comfortable wicker chairs and plants.

"This is where we all hang out," Carolyn said. "That

way we can eat, drink, and be merry without walking back and forth to the formal dining room. I hope you don't mind informality, Katy?"

"No. Not at all. My mother was very formal and I'm the opposite."

"That's good. Adam and Jayne are used to us, aren't you?"

"Yeah, we're used to you," Jayne said.

"Mike," Carolyn called from the door. "Come down here."

A tall, gangly teenager, who looked very much like a young edition of his father, appeared at the door. By the blinking of his eyes and the way he rubbed his peach fuzzy jaw, it seemed as if he'd just got out of bed. He said hello to Jayne and Adam.

"Mike. This is Katy, Adam's fiancée. Would you get their luggage from the car and take it to their rooms? Jayne's in her usual spot. I've put Adam and Katy in the front top bedroom." She glanced at them. "You are together, aren't you?"

Adam nodded. "That's fine."

Mike shyly shook hands with Katy. Jayne said she would help and disappeared with the boy.

"He gets taller every time," Adam remarked to Carolyn.

"Doesn't he? He's taller than his Dad. I've got some coffee on, if you want some."

They settled into chairs and Carolyn served them coffee. Katy let Adam and Carolyn converse, while she just soaked in the ambience of being in Rory Dean's home.

Mike and Jayne returned with Molly and Rory. Molly looked normal in shorts and a long white shirt and her father was dressed in similar attire.

The conversation over the casual lunch ranged from goats' milk to Molly's success. After lunch, Molly and Jayne left for the studio and Adam, Katy, Carolyn and Rory sat around in the atrium enjoying the warm sun and drinking Carolyn's extra strong coffee.

Katy was very much aware that Adam had known Rory and Carolyn for a long time and wondered if the couple had known Jayne's mother or if that had happened before they met.

Rory leaned forward with his arms resting on his knees. "Katy. Adam has passed your compositions on to Lilah and I've heard she's enthusiastic. She will be here for dinner tonight to meet you."

"That's great," Adam said. "This is an opportunity for Katy."

"Yes, that's true," Katy said, feeling awkward. The entire trouble with her marrying Adam was the continued perception that people might think she was using him.

After dinner they went to see the studio.

As they all walked down a paved footpath to the studio, Katy's excitement was subdued by her unease about using Adam's influence to help her career.

A red light glowed over the studio door.

"Molly and Jayne are working on a duet. We'll just interrupt," Rory said, and opened the door slightly. "Cool for us to come in?"

"Enter," Molly's voice said.

Jayne and Molly stood to one side as everyone looked around. Katy actually hoped she would hear Jayne sing, but the two girls seemed diffident and almost shy.

After the studio tour, they went to see the goat farming operation. Adam had seemed to make a joke of it, but it was a thriving business. Katy was rather impressed with Rory's investments. He certainly hadn't trashed his fortune and was building a legacy for his family.

Lilah, Bill and their daughter, Delilah, arrived later in the afternoon. Katy thought Lilah appeared much thinner in person. Bill, with sharp, small features and fair hair, equal in length to both his wife and daughter, didn't seem at all the type of man Katy would have picked for the beautiful Lilah. Delilah was precocious and pretty, appearing closer to seventeen than fourteen.

For dinner everyone remained casually dressed. Carolyn did all the cooking herself—a delicious dinner of chicken, salads and lots of fresh vegetables. Sitting around the table, Katy felt she should pinch herself once in a while. Here she was sharing a meal with three major recording stars, engaged to marry a celebrated music manager, and on the brink of a major change in her own career. She was sure she was soon going to wake up from the dream.

But she was still awake in the night beside Adam. This was no dream. Adam's lovemaking was a reality. Her love for him was real. She just felt anxious about the scope of her involvement with him.

# Chapter Sixteen

Laura was managing the planning of the wedding at Adam's house, and Katy was in continuous back and forth text messages with her soon to be sister-in-law. She ended up signing a contract for a smartphone that was easier to manage than her last ancient cell phone.

She told the landlord that she was moving.

"No problem," he said. "Always have someone ready to move in."

Movers were booked to take her belongings to Adam's house, but there was still a lot of packing to do. As well as making sure that the restaurant was running smoothly.

"Don't worry about it," Carol said. "We have lots of business and good staff."

"I don't want to leave you with the whole responsibility."

"I'm okay. I don't work at anything else like you do."

The weather was still warm and with Adam in Europe again Katy was always alone. So it cheered her up when Robert and Patty kept their promise to come to Toronto for a weekend.

Patty phoned as soon as the couple arrived at their

hotel on Friday evening. "We thought we'd come and visit you this evening. We'll bring some Chinese food in."

"Sounds great," Katy told her, and immediately she hung up the phone, she dashed around tidying the apartment as much as she could.

She put plates, wine glasses and a bottle of wine on to the kitchen table. The couple didn't take long to get there. Both wearing jeans and T-shirts they looked re-laxed away from the children for the weekend.

"This is a pleasure," Patty said as she helped Katy open the cartons of food. "I hope you like all this stuff."

"I'll eat anything after being on my own for so long," Katy told her.

Robert pulled the cork on the bottle of wine and sniffed. "Not bad wine for you, Katy."

"I splurged," she told them. "You know I've got some-thing to celebrate?" She held up her hand to display her ring.

"We did hear that you were engaged to Adam Ste-venson," Patty said.

Her brother smiled. "Congratulations, Katy. He seems like a good guy."

Patty grasped Katy's fingers and peered at the dia-monds. "Oh, it's beautiful, Katy. The guy must be load-ed."

"Of course he's loaded," Rob said. "Dad said he has a beautiful home."

"You'll see his house at my wedding," Katy promised. "We're getting married there."

They ate the food, discussed the success of Roland and Trish's wedding and the fact that the happy couple were now living up north in their dad's condo. And wasn't it a coincidence that Katy was also marrying into the family. Katy hadn't had a casual evening with her brother for so long, she felt really delighted the couple had made the effort to see her. But she wished Adam was here with her. Couples were supposed to be together to celebrate their love, not apart.

She made some coffee and they took it into the living room. Robert, always restless, checked out the bookshelves that were quickly emptying.

"Do you still have that *Rock Memories* book I gave you years ago, Katy?" he asked.

"Yes. It's on the third shelf down. I haven't got around to packing the big books yet."

He bent, perused the titles, then ran his fingers over the spines until he stopped and lifted out the heavy, glossy covered book. "I've learned something about Adam," he said. "You probably know, but …"

Rob moved to the sofa and placed the book on his knees. He began to leaf through the pages. "Why didn't you tell me, Katy? You know what I fan I was."

"You mean, Rachel?"

"You know they were together?"

"Jayne's her daughter, but just don't go telling everyone. Adam keeps it quiet for Jayne's sake."

Patty gasped. "Jayne is Rachel Frank's daughter?"

Kathy nodded.

"Here," Rob said, holding the book for Katy to see.

She sat down beside her brother and took the book. She looked down at the *In Loving Memory* section.

Robert's finger pointed at one photograph. Rachel had been a beautiful woman with perfect heart-shaped features, long black hair and in this picture she was wearing a floor length white dress accepting a Grammy award. She didn't appear as if she would eventually die of an overdose. Katy imagined Adam loving her.

Robert said, "Rick Salinas, the drummer was her boyfriend at this time. I can't believe that Adam was her boyfriend and Jayne is her daughter."

Patty added. "Rachel Frank is his idol. Imagine."

"Imagine," Katy said and closed the book. "Look, please keep this in the family. It's so long ago. And half the reason Adam is against Jayne pursuing a singing career."

"It must be all over the internet."

"It's not," Katy said. "I checked. Somehow he's really managed to keep himself and Jayne very private."

"Whatever. But it's exciting."

"It is exciting. Adam is exciting. This just adds to the mystique. But, despite all that, and this, I have to make sure I keep my feet planted well and truly on the ground and only see the man behind all that glitter."

"You seem to be forcing yourself to believe that," Patty said.

"No. Not forcing, but there is an aura of awe about him sometimes."

"I understand," Rob said. "But I hope you don't break the engagement."

"Even if I don't marry him, Rob, you'll still have Adam in the family."

"I suppose."

After her brother and his wife had left that evening Katy sent a text to Adam, just to make sure that they were still a couple. One came back saying, "I love you."

•

By the time Adam arrived at his office on Friday, Alison already had his schedule booked solid. A schedule he needed to evade. With a promise to be back later he drove downtown to Katy's apartment. He'd informed her when he was due home so she would probably be expecting him some time today. He was eager to see her again.

It was a hot day, with a rather depressing humidity factor. Adam unbuttoned his suit jacket as he walked along the tree-lined street. He found Katy, dressed in brief shorts and a blue halter, sitting on the front step outside her apartment talking to a neighbor. The neighbor was a huge hairy beast of a bearded man, dressed in black cargo pants and a sleeveless sweatshirt.

"Hi," the guy named Leo said when he was introduced to him. "How are you today?" Adam found his hand pumped hard by muscled strength.

"I'm fine," Adam said. He stifled his jealousy to see Katy casually sharing her life on the front step with this brute.

"I'll see you, Katy," Leo said. "If you need to borrow the car, holler."

"Thanks."

The man disappeared around the house.

"He lives in the other apartment," she explained as they walked inside and she closed the door. "He's a car mechanic. I borrow one of his cars once in a while. Now Heather's gone."

Adam could sense his absence had erected barriers between them. He loosened his tie and walked farther into the living room. "You won't need to borrow his cars from now on."

"Probably not." She looked at his features. "You look tired. Would you like some coffee?"

"Love some." Adam followed her into the kitchen.

He wanted to touch her but he felt as if she didn't want him to. He watched her prepare the coffee in her small coffee press. He liked the way she worked. Every action was efficient. There were little drops of perspiration on her brow and he realized she wasn't as cool and uncaring as she made out. He walked behind her, lifted her hair and kissed her shoulder. "I love you."

He felt her body convulse. "You've been gone so long it seems."

"I know. I'm sorry." Adam stroked her arm. This time her limbs went taut and he let go as if he had been burned. Feeling rejected he moved away from her and thrust his hands into his trouser pockets.

Katy stood with her back to the counter. "When you wear a suit," she said softly. "I always feel as if you're just here between meetings to grab a quickie."

"It's not true." Then he had to clear his throat to eliminate the fear accumulating like a hard knot in his chest.

She touched her neck with her hand as if she also hurt there. Then she turned around to hunt for mugs in one of the cupboards. She placed two glass coffee mugs on the table. "Do you want anything to eat?"

"No. Thank you. We'll go out for dinner."

She said quickly. "My brother and Patty were here last weekend to get away from the kids."

"That was company for you."

"Yes. It was. Rob's a music fan from way back. He used to be involved with different fan clubs."

Adam had the feeling she was trying to tell him something. "What does he want, Katy? Does he want to meet someone I represent? I'm sure I can manage to …"

"No." She cut him off. "That's not what I'm saying.

The person he would most like to meet is dead." She cleared her throat and said quickly, "Rachel."

"You told him?"

"No. He found out somehow that you were involved with her and I had to tell him that Jayne was her daughter. I told them to keep it in the family."

"Can we trust your brother?"

"I think so. Anyway, what would it matter?"

He sighed. "I guess it doesn't anymore. She was only singing in cheap clubs when I met her. She was older than me. I was staying in Florida with my father and his wife. I went to a club with some friends. She was on stage with a group called The Paupers. The guys I was with bet me I couldn't get a date with her. So I sent her a note and she returned the note with a time to meet her the next day. I met her on the beach." He shrugged his shoulders to ease tension. "She was interested and I was young and horny so we used to go to her hotel room. Needless to say I won the bet. Anyway, I had to go back to Toronto to university. But she kept in touch. She wanted me to be her manager and book gigs for her. So I took her on."

"You were still at university?"

"I was. And I started this business on the side. I got her some gigs in Toronto and New York. She was still raw but the potential was there. I think that's when I saw my own raw potential in picking winners. The Canadian music business was quite hot and I let my studies go and took on a few more clients. We still got together in hotel rooms when she was in town. Then one weekend she told me she was pregnant and that she didn't want the baby because she was poised on the edge of her big break."

"But she did have the baby?" Katy said.

Adam nodded. "Yes. Only because I made sure that she was going to be free of the child. My mother got a nanny for Jayne here in Toronto and occasionally I'd bring Rachel to see her. I didn't return to third year university. I had six clients, including Lilah and Rory, and Rachel. When her single *Flame* came out she got really big. I booked a North American tour for her, and then she went to Europe and the UK. She started to get rich and she made me rich. She only had another couple of hits before she was into drugs and booze full-time. I wasn't sleeping with her anymore. She was with other guys. And then one Saturday in New York after a performance she went back to her hotel room and never woke up the next morning."

"And you were there?"

"No. I wasn't. I was in Toronto with my mother and Jayne. Of course I went to her funeral in New York as her manager. And that was it. Somehow I'd managed to hide Jayne's existence. It wasn't a secret so much for me, as for Jayne. I didn't want her life to be a circus. I wanted her to live a normal childhood."

"I understand. And that's why you don't want Jayne in the music biz?"

"Exactly. However, I can see she's going in that direction, but it would be nice if she graduated from university first."

"Do you feel that way because you gave up your studies for Rachel?"

"No. Not really. I just think she should have her education."

"What about Rachel's parents?"

"She was from Atlanta. I think they were dead. No

one in her family came to the funeral."

"Very sad really."

"Yes. She was lonely but driven. She achieved what she wanted with my help and then paid the price." Adam picked up his coffee mug. "Maybe I didn't handle everything the right way, but I wasn't very old. She was supposed to be the mature one."

"She had a responsibility for that as well, Adam."

"I know, but she made me very rich. She left everything to me which I put in a trust for Jayne."

"Including the guitar I saw on your office wall."

"That's the one she played before she became famous."

"Adam, you blow my mind away."

"Why?"

"Because of everything."

"She was a sad person. It's nothing to be in awe of."

"I know." She smoothed his hair softly away from his forehead.

He felt her touch like an electric shock. "I love you, Katy."

"I love you, Adam." Her voice shook. "Kiss me."

He did and they made love. Then he took Katy out to dinner, and Adam went home quite late. Jayne was in the studio but he didn't disturb her. He went to the cocktail cabinet and poured himself a drink, then sat down and stretched out his legs and watched the outside lights glow on the dark forms of the shrubs and trees outside. He was pleased Katy knew about Rachel and her connection to Jayne.

For years he'd kept that story inside him and now it seemed as if the memories were still there but they were released rather like taking the cap off a pop bottle and letting the fizz subside. This didn't make him feel mellow. He rarely did. But he felt calmer, as if he were now ready, completely ready to marry Katy.

# Chapter Seventeen

"And do you Katy Lorraine Kerr take Adam Mark Stevenson to be your lawful wedded husband?"

"I do."

"And do you Adam Mark Stevenson take Katy Lorraine Kerr to be your lawful wedded wife?"

"I do."

Katy felt Adam's fingers firmly wrap around hers as they were congratulated by friends and relatives. She felt quite lovely today in her ankle-length white satin dress, with a low round neck and a chiffon overskirt, her hair entwined with daisies. Adam's approving glances enhanced her confidence.

Her father and Trish came over to them.

"This is what I call keeping it all in the family," Roland said with a deep laugh.

Trish hugged them both. "I think it's wonderful and so romantic that you met because of us."

Laura joined the family. "I always thought I would beat Adam to marriage."

"Jason might get the bug now," Adam said.

"Don't hold your breath." Laura laughed. "I'll go down in history as the longest ever engaged woman and

Katy can go down as the shortest."

Adam chuckled. "She had to look for a new place to live. So instead of hanging around all summer, we decided to go for it."

"I think it's wonderful," Laura said. "It keeps Katy well and truly in the family."

"Thank you for that compliment," Katy told her new sister-in-law.

She glanced around the other guests. A chosen few. From her own side Rob and Patty and the boys, Heather and Joe, and Carol, with her husband Don. From Adam's side Lilah, Bill and Delilah, Rory, Carolyn, Mike and Molly with her drummer friend Chad, Ty and his wife, Marie, Jayne and Liam the new guitar boyfriend, and Alison and Tom Fortune.

Alison looked slim and nervous in a silver dress, her pretty features disguised by lines of strain. Tom, a short, muscular, good looking man, had flown in from a tour for the wedding. He acted, as he sipped his drink, as if he were distinctly uncomfortable and needed more action. There was obvious friction between the couple.

Alison raised an eyebrow at Katy as Tom and Adam began to talk shop. "I hope you have more luck than I do in keeping your husband at home," Alison said wryly.

"Adam has vowed to make more time for his family," Katy told her.

Alison made a face. "Tom vowed that once when we had Peter. Five years later Peter barely knows what his dad looks like."

"Adam has already learned that with Jayne."

Alison glanced at Adam, who looked so handsome in his dark suit. "I don't mean to be a downer, but we hope he has." Then Alison smiled. "I shouldn't talk like this. It's your wedding day."

"It's okay. I'm realistic. And I'm busy as well."

"It pays to keep busy. Don't give up your own life."

Katy remembered Alison's observations as she shared a plate of food with her new husband. When this meal was over they were leaving for Adam's condo in Florida. It had been a rush to plan the wedding but Adam had given her every resource including Alison to deal with the arrangements. Her father had even presented her with help, a generous check—money he said her mother had put aside for Katy's wedding. Rob told her he got the same amount when he married and he'd used it to buy his house.

So now, even without being married to Adam, she was fairly well heeled. *From now on your life will be like this, Katy,* she told herself. *You'll have friends who have famous names and there will be money to buy time to make music. And Adam will be here beside you: Your strong, exciting man, your dream lover, to help you find the way out of the darkness.* Only, why did she still feel there were shadows lurking in corners? Or was it merely Alison's comment that made her feel unstable?

Adam grasped her hand. "Come on, wife. We still have some guest visiting to do."

Katy smiled and squeezed his fingers to reassure herself he was warm and real.

After the meal, Katy escaped into the house to change. She had her clothes ready in one of the spare bedrooms. Hanging over the closet door was her two piece ivory linen, going-away suit. She unhooked the suit and stood with it against her. She stared into her eyes and experienced the sensation that she was only going through the motions of the moment.

"Hey," Heather's voice said from the door. "I wanted to congratulate you."

Katy put down her suit and let her friend hug her. She felt tears squeeze from her eyes.

Heather laughed. "Katy. You're supposed to be happy."

"I am happy."

"Then look it. Come on. I'll help you dress."

"Since when have I ever needed help getting dressed?"

Heather placed her small gold purse on the bed and prepared to work. "On your wedding day, that's when."

•

The entire trip to Florida had been taken care of in meticulous detail by Alison. A limousine met them at Tampa Airport and drove them to a gated condominium estate set near a golf course and overlooking the Gulf of Mexico.

"Three bedrooms, four bathrooms, a kitchen, a living area," Katy said as she explored. "And a view of the beach and sea. Wow."

Adam smiled and pulled his navy blue tie loose from under his solid blue shirt. "There's a pool outside the living room slider windows."

"Well, what can I say?" Katy smiled.

He shucked his blazer and pushed his hands into the pockets of his gray slacks. "I have a car in the garage so we can tour around."

"Sounds great." Katy thought his eyes, usually so blue, appeared lighter, tired. He'd worked long hours to make time for his wedding and honeymoon.

And although Adam thought Jayne was cool about their marriage, Katy wasn't so sure. She could understand the girl's feelings. Jayne and Adam had been a twosome for a long time. She was sure even Adam felt the distance developing between the two of them. The desperate goodbye hug between father and daughter had made Katy cry. Therefore, she let him have his silent thoughts on their drive to the airport with Todd. It didn't matter to Katy because she really was worn out. Preparing a wedding at short notice had been hard work. She'd also had to move her belongings from the apartment at the same time. They had slipped into one of Adam's spare rooms easily and her piano was in the studio.

She rubbed her forehead. She wasn't exactly looking forward to returning home and sorting out her life—name changes, friends to be notified, and a husband, with a daughter. Rachel Frank's daughter was her stepdaughter.

Adam watched her, saying, "There is a restaurant close by. They also deliver food. I could get something, maybe some wine as well."

Katy thought some food and drink might loosen them up a little. "I wouldn't mind."

"I'll order." He picked up the menu.

Katy kept her eyes on his back, on his shirt tugging over his muscle, on his hair resting against his collar. She had begun this journey into love with a glimpse of his dynamic hair. And here she was, married to the man: Adam Stevenson. The man, who less than a year ago, she couldn't even get to see.

"Okay. Wine. What else?" he asked.

"A sandwich would be fine."

"Good." Adam picked up the phone and ordered the food and the wine to be delivered to the condo. He seemed to know the person he was talking to.

Katy sat down on the side of the bed and slipped her ivory high heeled pumps from her feet. She tossed them over to where one of her bags sat and reached up her skirt to remove her stockings.

"Hey. That's my job." Adam came to kneel at her feet. His strong hands made a slow journey of the hose down one leg, then the other. He placed his hands on each of her naked thighs and pressed his head in her lap. "Katy." She stroked his hair down his collar, felt her breathing quicken and lay back on the bed. He moved on top of her and they began to kiss the way she'd wanted to kiss him all day. It was difficult to believe that marriage was supposed to be romantic when the preparations and ceremony cramped the lovemaking that had led to the wedding in the first place. Katy returned his kisses with aching moist warmness as his hands made their way over her body beneath her skirt.

"That feels good."

"You sure do."

The buzzer rang.

Adam kissed her cheek. "I'll get that."

He let in the delivery person and waited until the food arrived. He gave the guy a generous tip.

They sat down in the armchairs to eat the meal.

"We'll get to bed yet," Adam promised.

"Promises," Katy said with a smile.

After they'd eaten Katy put down her glass and went over to him. He held her and she entwined her arms around his neck. "I love you Adam."

He kissed her mouth. "And I love you, Katy. Let's do it."

Adam's heartbeat increased as he slipped inside her

waiting warmth. Katy was like visiting an oasis after years in the desert. She had claimed his body and his heart.

•

Adam went into the house to disengage the security system and then dashed out to lift Katy off her feet.

"Welcome home," he said as he let her down in the foyer and kissed her.

With her hand smoothing his hair down his neck, Katy laughed. She hadn't seen Adam this relaxed since she'd met him. If that was her doing, then she felt she'd accomplished something. Tension had now diminished between them with walks on the beach, drives along the coast, and hours of passionate lovemaking. She was sure Adam loved her in the same heady way she loved him. Even a quick trip to visit his father hadn't brought about any tension. Adam's dad was a casual, bearded man who seemed pleased his son had found love.

"No one's home," Katy said as Adam collected the luggage and began walking up the stairs. She followed.

He glanced back at her. "Stella won't be back for a couple of days and Jayne's still with Molly."

"Seems like you told them all to stay away." Fur brushed her legs. "Except for these two."

He grinned. "They're no problem. We just have to remember to feed them."

Katy opened the French doors from the balcony in the master bedroom to freshen the air, and went to put her toiletry articles in the bathroom. Adam's bathroom was twice the size of any of the others in the house. There was a whirlpool bath, a huge corner shower, and a vanity counter containing three sinks and three oval mirrors. There were heated towel rails and a cupboard full of thick fluffy towels. It was luxury.

"Stuck on bathrooms?" Adam asked from the door.

"On yours in particular. It's so big."

"It's yours now," he said.

Katy turned around. "I didn't marry you because of all this, Adam. I married you for yourself. If you'd lived in an apartment downtown like the one I lived in, I would have married you."

He smiled lazily. "Sure you would, sweetheart." He came over to hold her in his arms.

His breath on her neck warmed her and made her want him again. The last time they'd made love had been before they left the condo. They'd held hands in the limousine. They had snuggled in the plane. They had kissed most of the way in the airport limo to this house. Now Adam's thighs were pressing into her once more and she could feel the hard need in him.

The phone in the bedroom rang.

Adam immediately pulled away and left her. Feeling apprehensive, Katy watched him pick up the phone.

"Hi, sweetie. Yes. We're home. Yeah, we had a great time. How are you?" He looked over at Katy and mouthed, "Jayne."

She knew who it was. She had to share her husband with his daughter. She'd known that.

Adam talked to Jayne for a few more minutes and hung up. "She'll be home tomorrow evening because she wants to see me before I leave town again."

"Good," Katy said and went to her suitcase and began unpacking. "Where are you going?"

"I have to make a quick trip to New York. Next week Dallas. After that Europe, you know how it is, Katy."

*New York, Dallas. Europe. You know how it is,*

*Katy.*

Feeling tears about to start, Katy walked into the closet that already contained a lot of her clothes, put there before the wedding. She was pleased the closet was large because she could hide in it. Possibly her agitation was caused by the world suddenly intruding on their pleasure, the looming business trips threatening a separation she wasn't sure she could handle.

"I'm going down to feed the cats and see what's to eat for us, Katy," Adam said. "Don't rush."

"Fine." She swallowed back the hot tears. She had no business crying. Everything would be fine. She would adjust.

Katy changed her navy pants and top for a pair of denim shorts and a black T-shirt and joined Adam downstairs, feeling the way she had the first weekend she had ever come to this house—like a guest.

Stella might not be here but her thoughtfulness was. The refrigerator, freezer and pantry were all filled with food. Adam prepared a salad, while Katy heated a homemade pan of Lasagna. After dinner, they walked in the garden, which had been kept neat and tidy by the landscapers. They went to bed early. Katy realized, as she slipped into sleep after some passionate lovemaking, that this would probably be the last night they were completely alone together in the house.

Adam's harsh voice woke her up. She lifted her head to see him pacing with his phone attached to her ear. Katy buried her head under the pillow, knowing that reality had to strike again sometime. She had to acknowledge that. She emerged from beneath the pillow as he was disconnecting the call.

"I thought we had the weekend together without a

phone call," she said, knowing she sounded accusing.

He raised an eyebrow. "Ah. Alison caught up with me." He placed the phone on to the dresser and crawled on to the bed with Katy. "Don't worry. We have today."

But for Katy their time together on Sunday was tainted by the prospect of the hours and minutes disappearing before Jayne came home. Because of the phone call this morning Adam was stuck in his study for the afternoon. Early evening Katy went up to their room and soaked in his big marble bath amongst perfumed bubbles.

Adam poked his head around the door. "Are you still with me?"

"I'm with you. Are you with me?"

He walked into the room and sat down on the wide edge of the bath. He wore only his jeans and his body looked hard and muscular. Very male. A stranger?

"Sorry. I got caught up in some stuff."

Adam stood up, unsnapped his jeans and eased out of them. He slipped into the tub with her. It was big enough for four, let alone two. He moved around the edge, and took Katy into his arms, facing him. He kissed her moist damp lips.

"I love you," he said.

"I love you as well. That's why I miss you when you're not with me."

"I can't help it. I deal with a lot of mercurial personalities." He kissed her nose, tightened his arms around her waist and insinuated his thigh between hers. "Don't be one of them."

"You mean I'm supposed to sit back, grin, and enjoy?"

"Yeah." His damp warm mouth brushed against hers

and she felt him hardening against her.

Adam drew her down on to him and the water sloshed and splashed as they strove for mutual pleasure. His mouth claimed hers over and over his hands clung to her hips. When the ecstasy struck, they both cried out in joy. They sank into the quickly disappearing bubbles. Adam stroked her wet hair and Katy lay in the bliss of the aftermath. She didn't want to think about the future.

But the future arrived later that evening when Jayne came home. Watching Adam hug his daughter, Katy knew she would always only ever have a part of him. It probably didn't help that Jayne wasn't young enough to be Katy's own daughter. She was a separate grown-up entity, almost a contemporary of Katy herself.

But Katy couldn't be angry with Jayne. She was a warm friendly girl and she hugged Katy as well. "You two look sooo good," she said.

"We had a wonderful time," Katy said truthfully. "Did you?"

"Great." Jayne sounded enigmatic and Katy figured she'd been pursuing her music without her father around to thwart her.

"Anyway, you two, I'm not going to get in the way. I'm thinking of moving down to the room next to the studio to give you space."

Remembering their noisy pleasure earlier in the bath, Katy felt that might be wise. She glanced at Adam.

He shrugged. "Whatever you want."

Jayne gave a whoop of joy. "I've waited years for you to say that, Dad."

"I only mean the room transfer."

"Sure. See you later guys."

"It's almost as if she knows what we're doing most of the time," Adam said.

"Of course she knows," Katy reminded himr. "She's not a baby. She's just about a grown woman."

"I know. I've been seeing it for the past year. It came suddenly. One minute she was still a teenager in school uniform at her private school, the next I saw her dressed up in high heels and a skimpy dress for some social."

"I wonder if my father ever felt that way about me."

"I'm sure he did. You should be good for Jayne. You're not that much older. You remember what it was like to be heading toward twenty."

"Yep." She grinned. "You won't like it."

"Ah. I can't talk. I was making love to her mother when I was nineteen in the back of a music group's van. And her mother was almost twenty six."

The words were spoken in jest but they still bit into Katy's confidence. She had lived a full life until now but she had missed so much of Adam's.

•

Even if she had given them privacy, Jayne's presence in the house was tangible. Adam acted reserved that night, and the following morning, Katy barely had time to run downstairs to wave and kiss Adam goodbye before Stella arrived.

*The Honeymoon is over,* Katy thought, tugging off her pyjamas and stepping under the shower. As the water pounded down on her well-loved flesh she wondered why she felt so low in spirits all the time. Adam loved her. Jayne seemed to have accepted their union.

She lived in this luxurious house. She had the music biz at her fingertips. She could compose songs all day long if she wanted to. Soon she would be working with

Lilah. *So what gives, Katy Kerr Stevenson? Why are you so blue?*

Determined to cheer up, she dressed in jeans and a top and went downstairs again.

Katy moved to help herself to a cup of coffee and a glass of orange juice. Instead, Stella did the chores for her and Katy only had to sit down on a stool and wait.

"You don't have to wait on me," Katy told Stella.

Stella placed a mug on the counter. "It's part of my job description. What would you like to eat?"

"Grapefruit and toast."

"Right." Stella went to prepare the food.

Jayne came in. "Mind if I join you, Katy? We'll be it while Dad's gone."

"At least there is plenty of recreation around this house," Katy said.

"True. Lots to do."

Stella put the half cut grapefruit and toast in front of Katy and poured coffee.

"What would you like Jayne?"

"I'll have the same. I have to watch my figure."

"Sure you do." Stella laughed and went away to get Jayne's request.

Jayne said, "We should go to the studio. I've never heard you play piano or any of your songs. And you haven't heard me sing yet."

"Do you think that would be okay with your father?"

"I'm not a little kid. He can't boss me around anymore."

"He knows that."

"Yeah. Sure. But it's cool he has you because I've realized that I get more time now I don't feel responsible for his happiness."

"Is that how you felt about him?"

"Yes."

Stella placed Jayne's food before her and Jayne dug out some fruit amongst the grapefruit juice. "At first I was jealous. I admit it. You were cute and pretty and Dad was hot for you. But now it's turned into love its okay. And I really didn't want to be here alone all summer. I liked going to stay with Grandma because I get to do what I want."

"She doesn't hold you back?"

"No way. She believes in everyone following their own trail in life. So does Dad really. But I can't live in a cage. Even if the media do find out whose daughter I am, I don't think anyone will care."

"Do you remember her?"

"No. Not at all. Only things I've read and pictures. And I've seen stuff online when she won her Grammy. It's just so sad she's not around anymore. I think I'd like her."

Katy blinked back tears. "He was so young himself."

"I know. He's told me a lot of how he felt. We've been very close. He's a good dad. Except when it came to my music. He just didn't want to know."

After breakfast they went along to the studio. Katy sat down at the piano and played a few chords of a new song she had been composing.

"What's that?" Jayne asked.

"It's called *My Dream Lover*. It's not finished. It's about a woman who falls head over heels in love with an image."

"Is that what you did with Dad?"

"Yes," Katy admitted. "I saw him leave a limousine and then I met him. It's been like a dream."

"So do you have any other songs?"

"That clear plastic box contains all my work."

Jayne was persistent. Katy wondered how Adam had ever got this far in stopping her ambition. They found Katy's scratchy music and lyrics and Jayne posted them on the music stand in front of her.

With Katy playing, Jayne stood by the piano and sang *My Dream Lover*.

Jayne was naturally talented and with a little coaching, it wouldn't take much to put her on a stage with a hit single.

"You're really good," she told Jayne when the song ended.

"Thank you. Want to hear something of my mother's?"

"Sure." Katy felt the more she knew about Rachel Frank, the less the woman would seem like a legend.

Jayne went to a music file and pulled out some sheet music. She placed it in front of Katy. The song was *Big Sir*, with an acknowledgement at the top that R. Frank had written the music and lyrics. It was a classic song about the one big love in a woman's life, recorded a few months before she'd died, and had become the signature tune of her death.

"Is this about your father?" Katy asked.

"No. It's not," Jayne said in a tight voice. "I think that's what hurt Dad so much. The man she was really in love with, a man she never had, was Rory Dean."

Katy felt the saying, her eyes popped out of her head, might be appropriate at that moment. "Rory?"

"Yep. Dad took him on as a client and my mother fell hard for him. She didn't have him of course. Rory was married to Carolyn and he didn't want anything to do with her. Rory hates anything to do with drugs and my mother was an addict long before Dad met her. You know that?"

Katy nodded. "Yes." And she reached out for Jayne's hand and held it, unsure why she really needed to, but she felt sorry for the girl who had to live with the knowledge of what her mother had been and how she'd died.

To Katy's surprise Jayne held on to her hand and began to cry. "I've always tried to make sense of her," she wept. "Uncle Rory and Aunty Carolyn have told me the most because they were more detached than Dad."

"I understand that."

Jayne wiped her eyes with her hand and sniffed. "This is silly."

"No. It's not silly. The first weekend I was here, your father showed me the studio and left me here. And I sat down at this piano and cried about my own mother's death for the first time."

"But I didn't know my mother."

"I didn't really know mine either," Katy said. "We just have to go on."

"I know," Jayne said. "So shall we get going on this?"

Katy played the first chord and Jayne began to sing. Katy never played another note. Jayne carried the song for all she was worth. She had obviously rehearsed it over and over again and in some ways she was better than Rachel had ever been. Katy forgot that this woman in front of her was her husband's daughter. When Jayne arrived at the abrupt poignant end, Katy applauded as if she'd heard the performance of her life.

"You're wonderful."

Jayne flipped her hair from her face and perspiration gleamed on her forehead. "I've sung it a lot with Molly."

"Are you telling me your father hasn't heard you do this?"

"He's heard me." Jayne leaned her hip on the piano. "He gets all in a twist and doesn't want me to use her material."

"As you said, he's protecting you."

"And he can't do that. I have to perform. That's who I am. Nothing else will work for me. You must feel that way about your music."

Katy nodded. "I do. Yes. Actually, I think if you recorded that again with more modern music technology you'd have a big hit on your hands."

"They'd know she was my mother then."

"You want that, don't you?"

Jayne nodded. "I do."

# Chapter Eighteen

To Katy's delight, Adam came home early. He handed her a bottle of champagne and kissed her. "From the staff. They didn't have time before the wedding."

She hugged the bottle. "So many wonderful things happening."

"One more thing," he said, and tucked a set of keys into her palm. "I picked up a car for you."

Katy looked down at the keys. "A car?"

"Come outside with me."

Katy placed the champagne on a table and walked out the door with him. In the driveway sat a silver BMW. "Adam," she said with dismay. "I didn't ask for this."

"It's your wedding present."

"Well, fine, but an entire car?"

He grinned. "I could have managed the steering wheel, I suppose."

She entwined her arms around his neck and let herself inhale the warm male smell of him. "I love you, Adam."

He held her hips. "And I love you. And I've missed you. Take me for a ride. In the car," he added, when he saw her cheeky expression. "Then we're going to drink the champers in bed."

Katy turned left at the bottom of the driveway and wound her way along the rural highway. Adam gave her directions at a sign reading, "Beaver Dam Creek." The road became narrower until they reached a fishing spot beside a small lake. One empty truck was parked to one side, but no fishermen were visible. When she parked, Adam drew her into his arms. They kissed softly for a long time until they were so aroused they had to stop.

"I want to make love to you," he whispered, his hands sliding down her hip to the edge of her shorts.

"I think we're too big for this car."

"Then let's go home."

Katy knew everyone was at home, but they managed to get through the front door without Stella or Jayne appearing. They ran up the stairs to their bedroom. Adam locked the door and pulled the heavy drapes across the balcony door. Katy began to undress and Adam did the same.

"I've been thinking about this all day," he told her as he knelt above her on the bed, naked and aroused.

His palms caressed her stomach and rose to her breasts and he bent his head and his tongue and mouth moved over her flesh until she cried out and lifted her hands to arouse him in the same agonizing way. He thrust inside her in an easy movement that was becoming familiar, but the heated tension they created would never be familiar to Katy. She was so much in love with this man she never wanted their couplings to end. Even when the release came, they clung together and she thought about tomorrow, when Adam would be on some trip or another and how much she would miss this intimacy with him.

After Adam was gone the following morning Katy planned a schedule. She would start each day with a swim and exercise in the gym. Then she would spend the mornings in the studio working on her music. If the music went well, she would stay there in the afternoon. If not, then she would shop, do chores, or visit friends. After all, she had a car now.

Katy also learned how Adam's house ran. Stella coordinated the show. The landscapers, house cleaners, window cleaners, even a piano tuner arrived one morning when Katy was working. He left his invoice with Stella, who had a household credit card to pay accounts. Katy didn't have to worry about anything. Which left her plenty of studio time. Although by mid-week she didn't feel she was getting anywhere. She needed a break and decided to get in touch with her friends and she invited Heather and Joe to come to the house on Friday evening.

Jayne was on her gap year and home today so she went to find her. She was reading on the patio. Katy slumped into a lounger. "The weather is hot."

"That's why I had a swim," Jayne said. "Hear from Dad?"

"He'll be home for the weekend."

"Terrific. He seems to be leaving himself more space lately."

"Yeah," Katy agreed, even though it didn't seem like it to her.

Jinx jumped on her lap and dug claws into her bare leg. Katy howled. Jayne laughed and so did Katy. At least they were relaxed together now.

Katy was thrilled when Heather and Joe arrived in

Heather's car late Friday. Heather wore a diamond ring and was now officially engaged to Joe, their wedding about six weeks away in mid-September.

Stella had prepared a meal for Katy to serve to her friends and Jayne had decided to go to Molly's until Saturday because Molly was leaving on her fledgling North American tour soon. Heather and Joe had been to the house for the wedding, but this time the three of them were completely alone and her friends were able to explore and exclaim to their hearts' content. While Heather yearned for a similar swimming pool, Joe lusted after the studio.

"How's this look?" he asked stroking a guitar.

"He treats guitars with more respect than me," Heather joked.

"No. I don't." Joe put down the guitar and kissed his fiancée's lips with his hand venturing down her hip. "You feel just as smooth."

Katy experienced a surge of nostalgia for Adam's presence. He'd only been gone a few days and would be returning later this evening, but she missed him so much she hurt inside.

"I'm going to serve drinks on the patio," she said with an abruptness she didn't really mean.

Heather and Joe parted, looking a little flushed.

After the drinks they moved to the dining room, where Stella had set up the table. Heather and Katy gathered in the kitchen to bring in the meal.

"Joe thinks you're going to be able to get Adam to help him," Heather said in a worried tone as she prepared the basket of fresh baked rolls.

"I might be able to. Let's give it some time. I just don't want to promise things that Adam can't deliver on."

"I know. And I understand. I've made sure Joe understands that you're not in this for the free ride or to get your friends free rides. When I met Adam at your wedding I saw how much you cared about him, and how much he cared about you."

"Thanks, Heather," Katy said, hoping her friend's observation about Adam was true. Each absence made her doubt their love.

·

Adam arrived at the airport in early evening. He called Alison from the limousine just before she left the office and told her he was going straight home. Anything pending he would handle on Monday before he went to Europe Tuesday.

"Lilah wants to sign that contract with Katy on Monday," Alison told him.

"Okay. I'll bring Katy in with me. And that's it?"

Alison said, "Pretty well. Except, Molly's off on her tour next week."

"That's why I was in Dallas, but Tom's going with her?"

"I'm well aware of that. I'm back to my mother babysitting Peter."

Tom's absence couldn't be helped so Adam didn't answer her distress. "Nothing else?"

"No."

"Good. Have a great weekend, love. Make the most of Tom."

"It's heartbreaking every time, Adam."

Adam wasn't up to this tonight. "Alison. We'll chat one day, okay?"

"All right. You have a nice weekend as well."

"Yeah. Bye." Adam hung up, leaned back in his seat and rubbed his jaw. He was tired, but as he saw the sun glitter on his new wedding ring he couldn't wait to be with Katy again.

As Todd maneuvered the limousine around a Chrysler Sebring to park in front of his door, Adam realized he wasn't going to be alone with her. When he was in the house, he went in search of the voices he heard. At his dining room table, Katy was pouring red wine into large glasses for Heather and Joe.

Disappointment made his stomach muscles clench. "Hi," he said abruptly, thinking of all the years of privacy he had cultivated that might now be destroyed.

When she saw him standing there, Katy rose from her chair, almost knocking it over. She caught the back. "Adam. You're home early." She sounded guilty.

"I decided not to go to the office," he told her, giving Heather and Joe a cursory smile, as they smiled tentatively back at him. He wasn't used to guests he hadn't invited to his house. "Where's Jayne?"

"She went to stay with Molly overnight. She'll be back in the morning."

"Okay." He let out a breath. "Don't let me disturb your dinner."

"Have you eaten?" Katy asked.

He met her brilliant green, anxious eyes. "No. I haven't. I'll go shower and change and I'll join you." He had to force a smile. Then he walked out of the dining room and took the stairs two at a time. He couldn't remove the swirling, sick feeling from his stomach. Even a shower didn't do it for him. He shaved, dried his hair and changed into casual slacks and a shirt. Then he went downstairs. Katy had set a place for him: At his own table.

"So how is everyone?" he asked as he sat down and Katy poured him a glass of wine.

Heather and Joe nodded and he could see he was making them nervous. Heather was an attractive woman and Adam quite liked her, and while Joe had never done anything to hurt him, Adam still didn't like the fact that he might have seen Katy in more than intimate circumstances.

"I'll get your dinner," she said. "Stella cooked a deep dish chicken pie that's really good and we're having it with salads. Sound okay?"

She placed her hand on his shoulder and he felt the heat of her attraction. He was nuts about her, vulnerability he hadn't really wanted. "Sounds good," he said casually, but he didn't touch her hand the way he wanted to.

Heather left the table to help Katy and Adam drank some wine. It wasn't his wine. Katy had obviously gone out and bought some bottles of her own. That was the way Katy was. She didn't want much from him at all. But he needed more from her even if he wasn't sure what it was he did want.

"How is it going?" he asked Joe.

"Great. I'm getting married soon."

"That's true. How's the music?"

"I've got some good gigs."

Adam nodded. "That's great news." He wondered if he should offer to meet with Joe. He was saved from that suggestion by Katy and Heather's return with the food.

He felt better after he'd eaten, but he wasn't too keen on entertaining Katy's friends. However, they didn't stay long and by nine they were leaving.

Adam returned through the front door with Katy. At last he was alone with her but she was tense and stiff.

"What did you do that for?" she asked him.

"Do what?"

"Act like you didn't want my friends here."

"I wanted to be with you alone."

"Well, you've just lost that chance." She swished through the foyer and out through the annex.

Adam followed her and caught her beside the pool.

"I wanted to be alone with you and I was disappointed when you weren't."

"You came home three hours earlier than you told me you would. Notice that Joe and Heather left at nine because they thought you were coming home at nine thirty.

He raked his fingers through his hair. "So I was expected to stay away from my own house?"

She made a face at him.

It was dark except for two outside lights. Katy stood in the glow, her hair silky, her skin like cream, her body in a tight little top and slim slacks, very slight and almost ethereal. He reached for her and she tugged aside, not letting him touch her.

"You can't treat my friends that way."

"I've kept myself private all these years."

"And you're still private as far as I can see. But this is my home now, you've told me that, so I can invite my friends here."

*What the hell*, he thought. *What am I doing? I'm being unreasonable, the way I am with Jayne sometimes.*

"I didn't mean to upset you."

"Well, you did, and now I am." She brushed her hand

through her hair and he heard her let out a sob. "I've always been kind of a lonely person inside and it's always made me rush into relationships with men. Not always sexual, sometimes just steady dating, but I—I think I made a mistake and rushed. I was stupid."

"No." The word tore from his throat and he stepped forward and clasped her into his arms. "No. Katy. No. This has been no mistake. I love you. I love you. I do. Just love me back, please."

He thought for a moment she was going to rip herself apart from him again, but instead her hands roughed up his hair, her mouth pressed hard to his, and her body wound around him. "Love me as well, Adam. I get so lonely without you. I miss you so much."

She was gasping for breath and so was he and he couldn't get out of his clothes quickly enough and neither could she. On one of the pool loungers they consummated their vows of love after an absence one more time.

•

Katy felt heavy-headed when she woke up. After their lovemaking they'd come upstairs and made love again, more gentle, softly caressing love this time. But sleep still hadn't come easy to either of them. Adam was restless from a week of high-powered business, and Katy was upset about his reaction to Joe and Heather being there. All the lovemaking in the world, she thought, tucking her head into the pillow, couldn't make up for the thoughtlessness of that reaction. That Adam was still jealous of Joe was no secret. She was sure Joe had sensed it.

When at last it was morning, Katy got up, slipped into cotton lounge pants and top, and pattered barefoot downstairs. Stella wouldn't be in today, and for that she was grateful. She just needed to be with Adam for a few hours until Jayne returned.

She rested her elbows on the counter top and buried her head in her hands. There were a lot of other aspects of her husband she didn't quite understand. That he was jealous and mistrustful of other men, she understood. Everyone was jealous. But he shouldn't be rude to her friends. She needed a life apart from his. Was this part of his problem with Jayne? Maybe the reason he held his daughter back from her performing was nothing to do with her mother, and all to do with Adam's own need to dominate and control. Once Jayne was outside these walls, he would lose that control. After all, he had built a little empire of his own. He was the boss.

She felt tears drip through her fingers. She really had thought she was a sophisticated woman of the world and had gone into this marriage with Adam with open eyes. Now she realized she wasn't sophisticated or knowledgeable about men the way she'd thought. She was at a complete loss as to what to do to make their relationship work.

She heard Adam's footsteps. "Are you making coffee?"

She snapped her head up straight and looked at him. He wore jeans and a shirt—a fit, healthy male, except his eyes seemed tired and baffled. "Yes. I am." She fumbled toward the coffeemaker.

"What's the matter?"

"I don't know yet."

"That's not like you. You usually have a pat answer."

She swung around. "Is that what you think about me?"

"You do seem to have answers for most things."

"Well, I don't. I don't have an answer for a relationship that has progressed into marriage. I don't know where to go from here." Katy drew a deep breath. "It's difficult, Adam, to keep a relationship together when you aren't here. If you had a normal job so that you came home every evening that might be fine. But it's not like that."

"I told you I'm trying to accommodate my family life. I've given you a lot of hours."

She plunked the coffee can down on the counter and pried open the lid. "Given me."

"Shared with you then."

"That sounds better." She dug into the coffee and left a trail of granules across the counter as she tossed the measure into the filter.

"Katy, surely you can handle your own company. You have your own work."

"Yes. I know." She poured in water and clicked the switch. "I'm being unreasonable."

"You sure are." He came up behind her and pressed his body into her. "Come on. We have such a good time together."

She leaned back into him and his arms came around her waist. She nestled into his comfort. "I guess it's that everything is strange. My life has changed more than yours."

He kissed her ear. "Are you making music?"

"Yes. I'm doing well. The studio is a super place to work."

"I'm pleased about that. Lilah wants to sign that contract on Monday morning in my office."

"Wonderful." And it was. She was the envy of a lot

of her musician friends. *So smarten up Katy, get your act together. What does it matter if Adam has hang-ups? All men have hang-ups. Women have hang-ups.* She had hang-ups.

She turned around in his arms and he parted her shirt and she unzipped his jeans. Lovemaking always seemed to have a calming effect on her but this time it didn't. She was sure Adam used it as a way to keep her under control and in her place. For the first time with Adam, she didn't give of her whole self and when it was over she turned away from him and ran upstairs, ignoring his cry to stop. She didn't want to be controlled. But she realized she was. She was always here, probably always would be here, waiting in his home for him to return.

# Chapter Nineteen

Katy signed her name on the contract beneath Lilah Payne's. Adam handed her a check, the money making the deal real, it also emphasized how hard she had to work. This amount of money didn't come for nothing.

When the business was taken care of, Katy went for lunch with Lilah and Adam. Lilah asked questions about her music and her compositions and Katy was forced to answer with observations she had never really considered about her work before. She'd often chatted to Joe and other friends about creativity, but she hadn't actually tried to make sense of the creative process. Lilah was now making her feel like a real working musician and she began to wonder if she was rising out of her own sphere. Could she compete with the Lilah Payne's of this world? Adam drove her home mid-afternoon because he had to get ready to go to London the following day.

"Don't be in awe of Lilah," he said as he turned into the driveway.

Katy wrinkled her nose. "Does it show?"

He smiled. "To me, but probably not to Lilah. She's usually got her head in the clouds."

"Is that why she seems abrupt and vague at times?"

"Possibly. But she's a perfectionist. You'll discover that."

When they were home, Katy helped Adam pack for the following day's flight. Following that they had dinner with Jayne. Stella served the meal in the dining room and the formality added an edge to the atmosphere. Adam was leaving tomorrow and he would be gone for three weeks until September.

Katy's mood turned to apprehension at being apart from Adam again and although Katy didn't mean to, she lay trembling in tears in his arms later in bed. She had so recently fallen in love and now he was leaving her. Again.

"I'm not leaving you," Adam told her, with kisses in her hair. "And isn't absence supposed to make the heart grow fonder?"

"Bull."

"My tender wife."

She couldn't help laughing. "I have to be hard on the surface otherwise I would crack myself up."

"I don't want to leave you either, if you want to know the truth, but I have no choice."

She didn't say anything because she felt that he did have a choice. It was called delegation. Instead, she positioned herself above him.

Adam flicked his tongue over her lips. "Are you going to make love to me?"

"I'm going to give you something to remember," she told him.

In the morning, Adam awoke still aroused. Katy's body had moved smoothly as silk against him last night, until he couldn't think of anything else but her scent and the way she claimed him as her own. He stumbled from the bed and stood beneath a cool shower. After the shower he leaned against the tiles and wondered where his brain was. Who in their right mind would keep leaving a wife like Katy after such a short time married?

He spent the next hour getting dressed and finishing his packing. When he went downstairs he found Katy and Jayne eating breakfast, so he sat with them and accepted Stella's toast and glass of orange juice.

"Everyone's in a good mood this morning," he said.

Jayne got up from her seat. "I'll leave you two to figure that one out."

Katy shrugged. "I just wish you would leave, and get it over with."

He put down his glass. "It hurts me to part from you as well, Katy."

"Possibly."

"Not possibly. It does."

She rose from her chair. "I'll see you before you leave. Let me know."

He felt like hell when he was in the limousine with the sweet taste of her mouth lingering upon his. He felt like hell when he was finally on the plane trying to make sense of a report from Donaldson. And then he realized he had people waiting on the other end, depending on him for their welfare. So he cleared his mind, as he had taught himself to do years before, and became what he was most successful at: Head honcho of SMM.

•

Katy wasn't even sure if she dressed appropriately to mix with musicians of Lilah's caliber. So she went to a shopping mall and purchased some trendy jeans, skirts and tops that would cost less in other stores, but possessed a designer label to make them acceptable in certain crowds. She spent the weekend with Jayne, wishing that Adam was here to accompany her to the studio on Monday morning. She was having a real huge case of nerves.

Jayne spotted the nerves. "Come with me," she said, taking hold of Katy's hand and almost dragging her into the studio. "We'll have a rehearsal. I'll be Lilah."

"Have you worked with Lilah?" Katy asked.

"I've been in on a few of her sessions. There were some times that Dad had to take me around with him when I was little. And she's been to the house."

Jayne dragged her hair down over her face. Then stood tall and straight. "So now I'm Lilah."

Katy laughed. "Okay. You're Lilah. So now what happens?"

"She has two male musicians."

"Okay. That's fine. I can deal with musicians."

"Good." Jayne walked over to the piano. "Now sit down, Katy."

"She'll do that?"

"She'll do that. She's bossy. She likes to control everything."

Katy sat down in front of the piano.

"We'll work on this one, *My Dream Lover*," Jayne said in a voice representing Lilah's sharp tones. "Give me a chord or two."

Katy did as Jayne/Lilah requested.

"No," Jayne said abruptly. "That's not what I want."

Katy kept her fingers poised on the keys. "You mean she's really going to be difficult to work with?"

"Yep. She'll be difficult. Her reputation is difficult, but the end product is good."

"You know so much," Katy said.

Jayne rolled her eyes. "I've been around these people all my life. I think like them. I want to be one of them. I'm going to be one of them."

"I think you already are," Katy said softly. "Okay, so what happens now that I haven't played the right chord for Lilah?"

"You'll probably go over different intros until you don't know one from the other, but eventually she'll find what she's looking for."

"Will I get any input?"

"Probably not the first time out, but argue with her if she doesn't seem to get it."

"Argue with Lilah Payne. Sure." Katy plunged her fingers down on the keyboard and played a melody from a popular song that wasn't her own.

Jayne listened. "You'll be fine," she said.

Katy trusted Jayne's intuition. Even so, she didn't feel very confident, when on Monday morning she dressed in a pair of soft jeans and a loose cotton top and drove her new car to Rory Dean's farm. She parked in front of the farm house and Carolyn was there to greet her.

"It's good to see you again, Katy. Aren't you excited about this chance?"

"Yes," Katy told her. She hoped no one thought she'd married Adam for this opportunity. But it sure looked that way.

Carolyn informed her that the musicians were setting up in the studio, so Katy walked along the path to the door. The occupied light wasn't on yet, so she pushed the door open.

Two men were working with equipment and they introduced themselves to her—Tate Styles on drums and

Max Lorense on guitar. Katy went to the piano and was warming up when Lilah arrived, wearing black pants and a green shirt. When she stood surveying the studio, Katy had to stifle a smile because Jayne's imitation had been spot on.

Lilah was all business. To add to her own compositions, Lilah had selected two of Katy's songs that Adam had given her, *Backward Love* and *Restless Lovers*. Katy understood why. Now hearing the lyrics come from Lilah's husky voice—she didn't really agree with Adam that her voice was sweet—and the melody formed by her guitar, Katy was rather stunned by her own songwriting ability. She could barely believe she had written those songs herself.

"Do you want to join me singing with the piano?" Lilah asked.

"If that's what you want?"

"Adam feels that I need some back up. Go ahead."

They performed the songs again with Katy singing the chorus with Lilah.

Lilah smiled at her. "I like that. Adam's right as usual. Do you have anything brand new?"

"I composed this recently," Katy said, running her fingers over the piano keys. "I called it, *Useless Words*."

Katy was nervous at first with Lilah sitting listening to her, but then she got into the song that was up-tempo and by the time she'd finished all she could hear was Lilah clapping and saying, "Bravo. I love that song. I'm going to use it. I might even call the CD *Useless Words*. We could make it my first single."

"It sounds good," Katy said, trying to keep her voice level and void of excitement while in reality she wanted to jump around and scream. This was the break she'd always wanted. She could say it was thanks to Adam, but really it went back to the coincidence of her father knowing Trish Stevenson all those years ago before Adam and Katy were even born. It was as if all roads led to this happiness—her marriage to a man she loved and her music coming to fruition. Then why the lingering uncertainty?

"Okay," Lilah glanced at her band mates. "Let's try one of these songs with all of us."

•

Each day from then on was taken up at Rory's studio. At first it seemed nothing would gel, and then gradually her music and lyrics began to sound as if she were hearing them on the radio. Despite the first impression she'd had of Ty as being jaded, he turned out to be a patient producer with a devilish sense of humor that even left Lilah smiling. Therefore, Lilah became less rigid as the days passed and Katy began to relax. Katy especially enjoyed the moments when Lilah recorded some songs of her own composition with nothing but her voice and an acoustic guitar. She felt privileged to be working with such talented people.

When Katy talked to Adam one morning she told him how things were going.

"So you're enjoying the big time?" he asked.

"I'm learning so much. Thank you."

"Your own talent really did it, you know."

"Plus a push from you."

"It's my pushes that cause things to happen. That's why I do what I do. That's what SMM is all about."

"I know that. Otherwise I wouldn't have come to SMM last December."

"You've been hot on my trail for a long time."

Katy thought his tone sounded a little taut, or maybe it was the phone line. She didn't want to cause any aggravation between them on a long distance phone call, so she let the hollow sensation in her stomach ride.

"How's Jayne?" he asked.

"She's fine. We're having a break, so I'm home for the weekend. It's her birthday."

"I know. I feel terrible about missing it. I hope you're going to celebrate with her?"

"Yes. We're going to spend the day downtown shopping."

"She should enjoy that."

"I'll make sure she will." No wonder Jayne had always been vocally bitter about her father's absences. Katy herself was beginning to feel the same bitterness. After two weeks away, even with emails, phone calls and texting, Adam was becoming distant from Katy. She was forming her own life alone without him. And this wasn't how married life should be.

She had lots to look forward to. She had to help Jayne celebrate her birthday. She liked Jayne immensely, and she would have done it for any friend the same way. To his credit, Adam sent heaps of flowers and other gifts that were delivered all times of the week.

As Jayne opened boxes of goodies, she said, "This is how I've celebrated a lot of birthdays with Dad. All my life it seems that I've had to grab each moment he's around. I really did think he might change with you."

"Maybe he hasn't had time yet," Katy said with hope in her voice.

Jayne shook her head. "Who knows?"

Katy held up a top Adam had sent Jayne from London. It was white, beautifully cut with a low round neck and long loose sleeves. "He did go out and choose this for you."

Jayne put her head to one side so that her long hair slid into a silky swathe over her shoulder. "Do you think he did, or did he just order a bunch of stuff?"

"I'd like to think he chose the gifts for you."

Jayne crushed wrapping paper into a plastic bag. "Did your dad buy you gifts?"

"No. My mother always bought them. My father's easier with giving us a check or a credit card to use."

"At least all fathers seem the same," Jayne said with resignation.

Later Katy drove Jayne into Toronto. They shopped for some birthday treats and ate lunch at a restaurant of Jayne's choice, which just happened to be Veggie Things.

"I wanted to see your restaurant," Jayne said as they went through the door.

They both had huge desserts. After all it was her birthday.

While they were at Veggie Things Katy went to the back to talk to Carol. "Are you okay without too much help?"

"We're doing great. Don't worry."

"You know," Katy said, "Adam suggested that we have entertainment here, maybe a piano player."

"You?"

"Well, he did suggest that, but I was thinking of giving his daughter Jayne a venue some time. We'll have to work something up, but I think it would be good for her."

"Okay, whatever," Carol said.

"I'll be in touch."

•

Even though it was a long weekend Katy went to Rory's studio on Monday for a heavy session with Lilah and her band. Jayne went out with friends if she wasn't spending time in the studio. Sometimes she stayed out late and Katy worried about Jayne for Adam and she wished he would come home. Finally, it seemed the day dawned when he would appear back in their lives. Katy had finished the studio work for a few weeks and it was Friday morning and busy around the house with the gardeners and the cleaners and Stella making sure everything was ready for Adam's return.

Stella left at noon, saying she thought Katy should be alone when Adam returned. Katy decided this was wise, she supposed, even if she felt as if her insides were tangled like spaghetti. She remembered her mother saying once, "Your father is coming home tonight, kids," and they'd all waited around the dinner table for Paul Kerr to walk in with his suitcase and his briefcase.

Katy knew Adam's flight came in about mid-afternoon. She showered and washed her hair and put on a long flowery skirt and a comfortable blouse. She fiddled with her hair and make-up for a long time then began to pace the house. When the phone rang she rushed to answer it.

"Is he home yet?" Jayne asked, calling from a noisy background of music and chat plus interference on her cell phone.

"No. Not yet."

"I'll call later to talk to him. Tell him that?"

"All right. I will. How's it going?"

"Great."

Katy hung up and sat staring at the dead phone for

a while. She missed having Jayne around. Another time she would phone Heather to chat but Heather was at work and besides, she was getting married next weekend. Adam had been invited to accompany Katy, but Katy wasn't sure if he would be around.

The cats wandered in and looked at her and she made a face. "This should be the most exciting time of my life," she said to them.

She checked the coolness of the wine, the dinner heating in the oven, the way the table was set for two in the dining room. She checked this all again before she heard the limousine in the driveway, the slam of doors, voices: Adam's and Todd's. Then the key was being turned in the lock and she walked forward to the door as if she really wasn't part of what was happening. Adam's travel-weary leather bags were tossed in first, then he came through the door. He closed the heavy door with a thud.

"You're hiding in the shadows," he said.

Katy didn't know what to say to him. He looked wonderful in a black leather jacket, black slacks and a white silky shirt. In fact he looked fine. As if nothing had happened to him emotionally over the past few weeks. No strain on his smooth skin, no dullness in his vital brown hair.

Nothing had happened to her either, except for her career taking off like a jet, and her emotions beginning to crumble like chalk. She didn't expect the anger that exploded from her like a flash of fire. She didn't expect to move out of the shadows and begin yelling at her husband. But she couldn't stop the outburst. She'd bottled everything up—lonely nights in this house without him, entertaining his daughter for him, beginning a new stage of her career without him.

Adam strode forward and gripped her arms. "Katy. Stop it. What the hell is wrong with you?"

Faced with Adam's features close to her, real now, after only being imagination for three weeks, made her calm down slightly. Maybe there were lines of strain beside his mouth and his eyes were slightly shadowed. Maybe he had suffered her absence. She shook her head, wanting to stop the anger rising any more. "What are you talking about?"

"Have you taken some drug?"

She realized that the concern was because she might turn out like Rachel. This knowledge made the anger boil over yet again. "Yeah, sure I'm into everything. I'm another Rachel Frank. Lord. If this is how you treated her, then hell, I understand her addiction."

"Her addiction had nothing to do with me. She was long gone before I even met her. Besides, I wasn't married to her. I'm presuming you're merely angry with me for being away."

"You presume right, Adam."

He let out a breath. "Don't even compare our relationship to the one I had with Rachel. I expected to come home to a loving woman, not this."

"How can I be a loving woman when I'm not being loved."

"I was only away for three weeks."

"During which time you missed your daughter's birthday. Not to say my work with Lilah Payne."

"Everything worked out okay, didn't it?"

"Of course." Katy felt exhausted all of a sudden. She ran her hand across her burning forehead. All her nerves thumped loudly through her system.

She saw Adam' mouth tighten.

Her shoulders slumped. *Talk about screwing up*, she thought.

"I'm going to shower and change and when I come down, I hope to have a nice peaceful evening with my wife."

He yanked one of his bags from the floor and took the stairs two at a time. In normal circumstances Katy would have followed him, but these weren't normal circumstances. Her outburst had made them abnormal. She had created a strain that didn't need to be there. But she couldn't back down. There were problems in their marriage. If Adam stayed home long enough they might be able to solve them.

# Chapter Twenty

Adam showered, ran an electric shaver over his jaw, and dressed in clean clothes. All the time he could sense Katy—her jars and tubes beside his in the bathroom, her clothes hanging to one side of the closet, her scent in the air.

He had expected to come home and be greeted in Katy's arms. Right this moment he should be making love with her. Instead she had shot off her mouth and now there was a huge problem between them he had to deal with, tonight of all nights.

He inhaled a deep breath, left the room, and moved easily down the stairs, pleased to be home but wishing circumstances were different. Katy was in the dining room, fiddling with silver cutlery on the table. She had seated them across from one another at the table.

Her shoulders were straight and tense, so he didn't approach her. He went to the big carved sideboard, selected a whiskey glass, and poured some of the amber liquid from the decanter. He drank it straight down and poured more.

"Talk about substance abuse," Katy murmured.

He turned around with the glass in his hand and

leaned his hips on the edge of the sideboard, even if he didn't feel as relaxed as he probably looked. "What do you expect?"

"Should I say I'm sorry or should we discuss why I'm so angry? I think we should discuss it."

He sighed. "Then I'll begin. Why are you so angry?"

She gazed at her hand holding a silver knife. "I don't really know, Adam. I just know that I exploded for some reason. It's like I was bottling stuff up. I'm not only angry for my own selfish needs, Adam. I'm also angry for Jayne. You missed her birthday. I think I began to see a pattern forming that I don't like."

"No one feels worse about missing Jayne's birthday than I do," he said honestly. "But she's used to me. And she knows these things can't be helped."

"That's what she said. But I'm not. I'm not used to being married and dumped in a house and left alone. This is a first for me."

Adam felt as if this was all too much to come home to. He was extremely tired from long meetings and negotiations. He hadn't had a rest or a break. He'd ended up with a quick wedding, a brief honeymoon, and then he'd returned full-force to the grindstone. To know that Katy was here at his home was difficult for him when he was away, because he wanted to be with her. And yet, there was part of him that was pleased to remove his presence because it left him less vulnerable. He was frightened of his vulnerabilities. He always had been. He got the feeling Katy was trying to make sense of him that way.

"Anyway," she said, finally laying down the knife on the linen tablecloth. "I have a meal ready for you."

"I'm hungry. That should please you."

She gave him a dark look. "Then sit down. I'll get the food."

He put his glass down on the sideboard and went through to the kitchen with her. He helped her carry the dishes into the dining room. She handed him the bottle of wine and he opened it for her. It could be like old times, he thought, except they didn't say much and they didn't laugh or kiss or touch. And what old times did they really have?

As they ate, Katy asked polite questions about his work and he answered them briefly, because now that everything was settled overseas he wanted to forget about it. Then he asked her how things were going with Lilah and she told him that they were pretty well finished except for a few more sessions.

"How's the car?" he asked, picking up his wine glass.

"It runs fine. Great."

"Good. So what did you do for Jayne's birthday?"

"We went into Toronto, shopped and went for lunch."

"Did she enjoy herself?"

"Yes. She did. Very much."

"So you two are getting along well?"

"Yes. We are."

Katy met his eyes with her brilliant green ones and he noticed they glittered with unshed tears. This wasn't what he had planned when he'd married her. But what had he planned? He hadn't planned anything. All he'd seen was Katy and the vital need to have her with him at all times. But he wasn't with her at all times. He hadn't made himself available.

He sipped his wine, replaced the glass on the table and picked up his fork to eat some salad with the tender meat and vegetables she had served. "I'm pleased you and Jayne get along. That's good."

"I'm sure you are," she said sarcastically. "It seems to me I'm here because Jayne couldn't be with your mom for the summer and you were at a loss."

"No. That's not the reason. She can stay here alone now."

Katy wasn't going to give up on him. "But you don't want her here alone. Not really. Yet she is alone. You've raised an independent woman, who lives half of her life without you knowing what's going on."

"What are you talking about now?"

"Her music. She's a consummate performer, Adam. You can't stop her."

"Did I ask to discuss this tonight?"

"No. But it's part of what's wrong with you."

"You're an expert on what's wrong with people, I presume." He didn't want to be so confrontational but he couldn't stop himself.

"No. I'm not. But I've noticed that you like to control your environment."

"Possibly," he agreed. "When my father left home, my world got messy. We had to move from the house and shack up in a two-bedroom apartment. Laura had the second bedroom and I had to sleep on the living room sofa bed. It wasn't ideal. I promised myself that when I was on my own I'd keep my life in order."

"Did that promise work?"

He twisted his lips in a wry expression. "It almost went off the rails with Rachel, but after her it's worked. Luckily Jayne's more like my own mother when she was younger. However, I don't like to be too cluttered up with emotional problems. I admit that. Right now I just want to be in love and not have to deal with anything truly heavy."

She put down her knife and fork and placed them together on the plate, her meal was barely touched. She rose from the table and left him alone.

Katy walked across the lawn. The air was crisply cool this evening, typical September weather, with the sun still glimmering through the trees. She wrapped her arms around her middle to ward off the wind that felt cool after weeks of hot summer air. Her mother had once said, "It's best to let it ride, forget it, keep the peace."

Well, maybe that had been her mother's way. But it wasn't Katy's. She had always tried to face her problems head-on. But this one was more ingrained, more tangled, a mess. It might take time to emerge from, very much like the grief when her mother died. It had taken until this summer for her to handle that and to feel more at peace.

When she felt cold, she returned to the house. Adam had cleared the table and the dishes. The kitchen looked spotless, all the untouched food put away in the refrigerator. She didn't have to look far to find him. He was in his study, on the phone. So she left him there and went upstairs. She took her robe, nightgown and toiletry articles from their room and bathroom and went along to one of the guest bedrooms. It was a pretty blue and white room with no connection for Katy to anything.

Adam found her there, bathed, wearing her nightgown and robe, sitting on the bed, brushing her hair. He held the top of the door as he looked at her. "What are you doing?"

"Getting ready for bed," she said tightly.

"Katy, don't do this to me. Don't punish me."

"I'm not punishing you. I'm trying for some distance from you."

"You have distance from me all the time. That's what our problem is, isn't it?"

"No. It's more than that."

Adam's heart thumped hard with unreasonable annoyance. He knew if he stayed here with her he would explode the same way she'd exploded, and he realized how rigidly he'd been holding on to his control over the years and how much Katy's presence in his life was beginning to unravel those tightly coiled emotions.

He couldn't speak. He merely turned around and walked through the open door and into the other bedroom. He sat down hard on the side of the bed and buried his face in his hands. He felt his shoulders begin to shake.

•

Jayne was home the next morning. An extra person in the house changed the dynamics between Katy and Adam. Jayne had so much to tell her father that Katy really didn't have to participate in most of the conversations. Meals were eaten casually. Dinner was a barbecue on the patio, with Adam tossing the burgers. It was bed time when Katy began to feel the pressure mount. She'd stayed apart from him last night. She'd caused a rift. She wished in her heart, she hadn't acted in anger when he'd come home. She should have put on the act as the sweet little wife-in-waiting and everything would be fine, except that would have been a sham to perpetuate a situation that was seriously flawed.

That Adam had admitted only wanting the joy of the love and not the reality made her feel extra blue. Until he desired the entire relationship, good, bad, evil, rotten and fun, it wouldn't be suitable for Katy. Now she was beginning to see how her realist nature had messed up many relationships with men, because she wanted the truth, the honesty that those men had been unable to give her.

What had she done by making waves? She had created more than a mere gulf that she couldn't possibly walk across, she had created an iron fence. Had he only loved her when she'd been willing and malleable? Didn't he love her as a woman who demanded straightforward answers from her man? A woman who wanted an equal partnership?

When they were alone later he asked her if she would stay in their room tonight, as Jayne was home. He didn't want her knowing anything was wrong.

"She might have sensed it by now, anyway," Katy said.

"Nothing is wrong for me, Katy. I love you."

"It's not enough."

"What more do you want?"

"I want all of you. I want the part of you that was a little boy. I want you as a teenager. I want all the dregs left over from all your relationships. Everything. The same way as I'm prepared to give you everything."

She saw now that his skin looked flushed and his eyes were red and tired. He wasn't taking this as easily as she thought he was. She was pushing him hard, maybe too hard. So she backed off slightly.

"All right. I'll sleep with you."

But that night Katy had no real deep sleep and got up in the morning with a headache. She found Adam and Jayne in the pool when she went downstairs. She slumped along to the kitchen for some coffee and played with the cats for a while. She always felt left out when Jayne was here anyway. But she couldn't believe the tension that had built up inside her. It was as if all her nerves were close to the surface of her skin. And why? All because of a man she'd thought was her dream man.

She hadn't learned her lesson. She'd repeated her faults and created expectations again. Dream men didn't exist. Only real men. Adam was proving to be as real as any man. But she still loved him.

Adam and Jayne came into the kitchen, both now dressed in jeans and T-shirts, their hair damp.

"You should've come in swimming with us," Jayne said, helping herself to a big glass of orange juice. "Juice, Dad?"

"Sure," Adam said, and perched near Katy. "Okay?" he asked softly. "You look tired."

"I am tired," she said honestly.

"Do you want juice, Katy?" Jayne asked.

"Yes. Thank you."

Glasses were placed in front of Adam and Katy. Jayne left them alone.

"Katy, don't let's wreck our whole lives because of one disagreement."

"It's not a disagreement. It's a fatal error."

He let out a breath. "For me to solve, it seems."

Katy decided she had to be honest. She couldn't be like her mother and never contest the problems. "It's not for you alone to solve. I can help, but first you have to sort out something inside yourself, Adam. I believe you really do love me. But you have to show love, Adam. And not with gifts and toys. It just doesn't work that way. At least not for me."

"I can't do much about it right now. I have to be in New York tomorrow afternoon."

"That's just great, Adam. You get out of your problems by leaving."

"I don't want to leave."

"I'm not so sure about that," Katy told him.

•

The next afternoon, Katy sat in the studio and worked out a melody for a new song, knowing that Adam was now at the airport boarding a plane. She was waiting, here alone, while Adam dealt with whatever crisis might be looming at SMM. It was either a pattern she would have to get used to, or a pattern she could leave behind by admitting she had made a mistake and this life with Adam was not for her.

Adam was still away by the following weekend and it meant that Katy was forced to attend Heather and Joe's wedding alone. Excuses were made for Adam, but she could see Heather's pity in her eyes. She was in the same situation she'd been in with Ken, except this was worse. She had married Adam.

"If it's for love, then that's what marriage is all about, isn't it?"

Hadn't Adam once told her that?

Well, Adam, she told the mirror in their bathroom on the eve of her friends' wedding. It's also about being together.

At least there was some solace in his house. She spent many hours in the gym using the weights and pedaling the stationary bicycle. Morning and evening she made a routine of the pool. Her mind clear from the exercise, she wrote songs about broken love, broken promises, and heartache, songs about expectations that never materialized.

The weather was growing dark and dismal. Drizzle pattered against the windows of the living room this afternoon and Katy glanced around the immaculate home and actually felt nostalgia for the clutter she used to live in. The mornings were fine when she was involved in her music. She didn't want interruptions then. Days were also pleasant when Stella was around. It was later on as the evening drew in and she knew he wouldn't be home when she began to feel unreasonably alone. At least when she'd lived in the city, she had her friends.

She was so alone that it was quite a surprise when Laura came over one afternoon.

"I hope I'm not interrupting anything," Adam's sister said as Katy poured tea.

"No. I've finished work for the day. It's good to see you."

"Hasn't Adam been home for a while?"

"He dashed in for a couple of days, and Jayne came home to see him, but that's all." Katy forced a bright smile. "Let's take our tea into the other room. It's nice and sunny in there."

"How's Jason?" she asked when they were settled.

"He's fine. Busy at work. I don't see him very often. I'm busy at work as well, now school has started again."

Katy thought that Laura seemed brittle over Jason in the same way she was brittle over Adam. Both men had deep emotional troubles. She at least knew the derivation of Adam's. Laura didn't seem to have a clue why Jason was so difficult to communicate with.

"Why do you stay with him?" Katy asked. If she had known a man since she was sixteen, who had actually tried to leave her a few times, she wouldn't be in Laura's position now. She would have been gone years ago.

"I love him. I really do. He needs me."

"Has he told you that?"

"Not in so many words, but we have an understanding." Laura finished her wine. "It's one of those long, complex relationships, where we part and come back together again over the years."

"Was it his idea to get engaged?"

"It was more a mutual thing. It's the next step."

Or the final step into hell, Katy thought after Laura was gone and she rinsed cups. Possibly Laura was like Adam. She liked her life controlled and a steady relationship in the background kept her life in order.

Not long after Laura left, Jayne came into the house, looking wonderfully familiar with her backpack and jeans. Jayne seemed just as thrilled to see Katy because she gave Katy a hug.

•

Adam heard music when he entered the front door.

Leaving his luggage piled in the foyer he walked through to the annex and listened at the open door. Jayne sang to Katy's expert piano accompaniment, a song he had never heard before, the melody taut and gut-wrenching.

Jayne stopped singing touched Katy's shoulder and Katy lifted her fingers abruptly from the keys. He thought they both looked guilty.

"Hi. Dad," Jayne said at last breaking rather a tight silence. "We're rehearsing."

"Are you using Katy's music?"

"Yes. Her music works with my voice."

"That's good," he said, even though he wasn't sure if

he meant the words. Katy's gaze didn't quite meet his, and he felt raw inside. He knew he was at a big intersection and the choices were going to be painful. His little girl would be leaving him. His wife might not want him if he couldn't open up his feelings the way she had begged him to. "Anyway. I'm home for the weekend. But I'll leave you two to get on."

He closed the door behind him and went upstairs to his room. He showered and changed into jeans and a sweatshirt. When he came downstairs the studio was still occupied. He felt like an outsider. Jayne had always been so eager to have him home. Katy had missed him most times. So what was happening? He felt as if they'd ganged up against him.

He strode through to the kitchen and found a beer in the refrigerator. He popped the cap and drank from the bottle. He had to think. Think about Jayne. About Katy. Think hard. Because something had gone drastically wrong. Adam was on his second beer by the time Katy came into the kitchen.

"Do you want dinner?" she asked.

"Where's Stella?"

"I gave her a few days off. Jayne and I had some work to pursue. We like being alone when we rehearse."

"You do?"

"Yes. We do." She still didn't meet his eyes. He watched her walk to the refrigerator. She wore a pair of faded jeans and a black top and her hair was tied back off her face with a black velvet ribbon. He thought her skin appeared pale and there were fragile blue shadows around her eyes. She tugged out a bottle of beer, pulled the cap off with the opener on the front of the door and drank from the bottle.

He recalled the moment in the kitchen at the lake when they'd shared another beer, but that time they had been full of lust for one another. He glanced away from her to the darkening late October garden. He was still full of lust for her, but his insides also felt twisted up. He ached desperately for her to smile and change the situation. He was sure that was all it would take.

He sat astride a stool. "Aren't you pleased to see me back, Katy?"

She leaned against the counter and rolled the bottle around between her hands. "You come and go, Adam. I can't keep feeling high one day because you're home and low the next because you're going away again."

"So, what are you feeling?"

She raised an eyebrow. "I'm not really sure."

"I'm going to be home for a few days. Let's try to set the situation right."

It was a very awkward few days for Katy, with Adam trying to be considerate. But they never made love. There was a definite barrier between them. And Katy knew she had put it there by making waves and forcing Adam to face up to realities he might never want to acknowledge. It was actually a relief when they had a surprise visit from her father and Adam's mother one morning.

"We hoped you would be home," Trish said, giving Katy a hug. She glanced over at her son. "I can't believe you're home as well, Adam."

Adam shook Paul's hand. "I'm taking some time off. I've worked long hours lately."

"It's nice you have Katy at home now to make you slow down." Trish smiled at her daughter-in-law. "And how's your career coming, Katy? I hear Lilah is releasing a lot of your music on her next record."

"Yes. She is. We've been working together. I'm playing piano on some of the recordings."

"That's wonderful news. Now, you two, get dressed up. We're going to take you to lunch at a nice little country place we know of. And then we're going to stay the night, if you don't mind, and pop out for a round of golf in the morning."

Katy found her father to be a different man with Trish than he'd been with her mother. He was loving, kind, gentle, sweet. He paid attention to her. He even succumbed with humorous resignation when she beat his par on the sixth hole the following morning. Adam let himself relax as well and the four of them had what Katy thought was a really pleasant time, a family time. But she knew it was only a temporary reprieve. Eventually she was going to have to face Adam with an ultimatum.

They were just drifting off to sleep that night when Adam's cell phone rang. Adam left the bed and Katy leaned over to switch on the light. She watched worry lines etch his brow as he listened. "Okay. I'll deal with it. Get Gary to take over for a couple of days. I'll be there as soon as possible. Call Amanda to take over from you. I understand. Take care, love. Bye."

He replaced the receiver and looked at Katy. "Alison's husband Tom has been taken ill in Dallas, during the Molly Dean tour. He's being flown home tonight."

"Oh, no. What's wrong with him?"

Adam raked a shaky hand through his hair. "Heart attack."

Katy felt shocked. "But he's only a young man, Adam?"

"My age," Adam confirmed.

"That's terrible, Adam. How worrying for Alison. Oh, dear. What can we do?"

Adam let out a breath and Katy saw his cheeks were drawn and pale beneath his tan. "You don't have to do anything. I have to see Alison. She's been my assistant since she was quite young, before she married Tom. It was my fault they met."

Katy ignored the hurt caused by his not wanting her help. "Fault?"

Adam shook his head. "It hasn't been a marriage made in heaven. Tom's never there." Adam walked towards the bathroom. "I'm going to meet Alison at the hospital for Tom's arrival."

Katy slumped back in bed. He didn't want her support. But poor Alison. At her wedding Alison had acted like a woman whose marriage was on the rocks, but for her young husband to have a heart attack was tragic.

One aspect Katy was very aware of, as she ate breakfast alone, was that Adam kept each of their routines and careers separate. He had given her the chance with Lilah, but he had offered no further input. It was as if he didn't want to get too emotionally close to her.

Shut out. That's how Katy felt as she paced the entire house in frustration, wishing she knew what was going on at the hospital with Tom. What if he died? Wouldn't Adam need her comfort? She could help Alison with Peter. If only he'd call her and ask her to be there with him.

# Chapter Twenty-One

Adam gave Alison a hug.

"Thanks, Adam." She was pale and shaky, but the tears had dried up.

"Take it easy," he told her before leaving the hospital room and walking down the long sterile hallway.

Tom's distorted suddenly-aged features remained with him. Tom went way back with Adam. They'd played football together when they were kids. When he'd started SMM he'd hired Tom for his organizational and leadership qualities. Tom worked conscientiously, and Adam had given him more and more responsibility, but he certainly hadn't meant for Tom to work himself into an early grave.

It was relief to feel the fresh, damp air after the cloying hospital atmosphere. Barely aware of his actions, he drove to SMM and found his office being run efficiently by Amanda, who sometimes worked on reception downstairs.

"How is Tom?" Amanda asked.

"He'll survive but he'll have to watch himself from now on."

"Alison will get her wish for him to stay home,"

Amanda said.

"True." All of a sudden he wanted to be alone. "Leave me alone for a second. No calls."

"All right." Amanda closed his door.

Adam rose to his feet and stuck his hands into his jeans' back pockets. He stared out of the window at the parking lot. Tom had almost died in Dallas. Fast medical action had given him this chance for recovery. Adam felt the welling of emotion through his chest and his eyes dampened. He never realized how close he was to his friends until something happened to them. He'd almost lost Tom. Alison had almost lost Tom. Little Peter had almost lost his father.

He clenched his fists. Alison told him that the doctor had said Tom needed to slow down. His work pace was beyond reason. He was to take at least six months off at home with his family and then they might give him a heart bypass. Adam had just given Alison and Tom carte blanche to do whatever they wished. Given.

His eyes focused on a tree swaying in the breeze. Isn't that what Katy accused him of? He gave to those he cared about. But he didn't take much. He didn't share. He kept himself to himself. Much like Tom had done. That's why they got along. They were similar in nature. They didn't need much to exist.

Or did they? Maybe they needed more than they thought they did. Tom's workaholic nature was, like his own, a way of hiding from the complexities of life and his relationships. Tom had always liked being single. When he married Alison, he had referred to himself as being captured. When Peter was born, he told Adam he felt the responsibility of a child like a noose around his neck. Adam had never felt that way about Jayne. He had cared deeply about her from the start, but he knew he had let his parental responsibility run to over work. He knew he could easily follow Tom down the same path to a stress related illness.

He rubbed his hand over his face. *Talk about a mortality check,* he thought. He remembered he was due in Texas tonight, which meant he still had to continue on his own treadmill. And he would have to leave Katy again in the midst of a strained relationship. He felt as if he were running uphill all of a sudden, and placed his hand over his pounding heart. Katy was waiting at the top of that hill for him to make a decision about their life together.

He decided to go home and talk to Katy. Maybe she would be willing to start again when he returned. But she wasn't at home. She had left a note saying she had taken Jayne somewhere. So he packed alone, left a scribbled note on the bottom of hers to say that he would contact her from Dallas later, and went with Todd in the limo to the airport.

Katy returned to an empty house. She had left Jayne with a friend in Toronto. She found Adam's note. *Gone again,* she thought, and her heart felt empty, as if she had no feelings anymore. She had always felt she wouldn't be able to walk out on Adam, but with this void inside her, she obviously could.

She couldn't even make herself feel alive in a warm whirlpool tub. She didn't even cry later in bed. She lay awake, staring at the ceiling, knowing she couldn't stay here much longer.

Alison phoned in a few days to tell her Tom was home. Feeling she should do something, she went to see how Tom was. They lived in a ranch style bungalow on half an acre not far from Adam's office. Tom was tucked into a comfortable chair with a blanket.

"I'm forced to rest," he informed Katy, his fingers clutching around the arm of the chair, as if he still felt he should be somewhere else doing something else.

"You haven't got much choice, have you?" she said sympathetically. His skin was yellowish and he still didn't look well in her opinion.

He shook his head. "No. I haven't. Did Adam get off?"

"Don't worry yourself about Adam," Alison told him, adjusting her pillow. "Everything will be fine at SMM. You're not indispensable."

"No. I suppose not." Tom grinned lopsidedly at Katy. "Look after Adam, Katy. Don't let this happen to him. It's not nice. It's damn scary." He leaned his head back on the pillow. "Oh, hell. It's exhausting even talking."

"Then don't, honey." Alison stroked his hair. "When I've seen Katy off, I'll help you in to bed."

"He's really sick," Katy said anxiously as she got ready to leave.

Alison walked her to her car, with Peter zooming around behind them pretending to be a NASCAR driver. "The doctor says he'll get better if he just quits smoking and eats a healthy diet and doesn't run himself quite so ragged at work. There's also talk of a by-pass. Yet in a way, this is a relief. We've been climbing a steep hill for a long time in our marriage and we're at last getting some time to talk and work things out."

It was a shame Tom had to almost lose his life for them to find time, Katy thought as she drove home. She was sure Tom's heart attack must have had a profound affect on Adam, but he hadn't made himself available to share any of that with her.

Katy was scheduled to spend more time with Lilah and she threw herself into her music, discovering her musical confidence was growing. Because of Lilah's interest in her work she was able to dissect her creative processes. This helped when Jayne came home on the weekend. They spent the hours in the studio, Jayne putting Katy's lyrics and music into vocals. They worked well together, almost as if they had a second sense of one another's intuition and talents. If nothing else came of her relationship with Adam, Katy decided, she had given Jayne a chance to showcase her talents. She just hoped that Adam wouldn't stop Jayne's development. She didn't want to have to fight with him about his daughter. She didn't want to have to fight with him, ever again.

She pursued an evening of entertainment at Veggie Things. She had a piano brought in and some speakers. Jayne was excited. "You mean I'm going to perform?"

"Friday night," Katy said. "I'll play the piano and you can sing."

"Thank you," Jayne said. "Thank you."

Katy decided that when she was in the city on Friday to perform with Jayne at the restaurant, she would stay the weekend with Heather and Joe. From there she would decide on what direction her life would take.

•

Adam arrived home from Dallas on Friday. Gary could run Molly's tour from now on. He checked with Alison, and found out Tom was at home relaxing. Life was calming down to normal. When he got home, he found only Stella at his house.

"Katy's gone downtown with Jayne," Stella told him.

"Do you know where?"

Stella sighed. "I did promise not to tell you."

"Why? What is it?"

"Nothing serious, Adam. At least not horribly serious. Jayne's performing at Katy's restaurant tonight."

He had spent so many years fighting Jayne that he actually felt shaky. "Whose idea was it?"

Stella shook her head. "It's not really for me to say much, Adam."

"Of course not."

"Laura is going along as well. For support."

He could hear the accusation insinuating he had never given support.

"Are you going to go and see her?" Stella asked.

He knew he should. The time had come for his support. He'd known it would eventually. And he wanted to see Katy so badly, he hurt inside. If he didn't reach out to either woman he would lose both of them.

•

"I've got the jitters," Jayne said, sitting at the table they all shared, and putting her hand out to illustrate the tremble in her fingers.

"You'll be terrific," Katy reassured her, wishing that every move she made lately didn't seem like she were performing at a distance. Or was that just because she was disassociating herself from her marriage? Soon, she would be on her own again. A divorce should be easy enough to get.

"I'm so looking forward to this moment," Laura told her. "I want you to go up there and wow the audience."

"If only Dad could see me," Jayne said.

"It would be great," Katy agreed. "But he's busy." She didn't add, doing other things so he doesn't have to face up to the people in his life. She was angry with Adam for missing this moment, for not being here for the chance to experience his daughter's talent. She was also angry with Adam for not working at their marriage, for assuming she would wait in the background.

Jayne stood up and tapped Katy on the shoulder. "Come on."

Katy thought she looked beautiful. Her eyes shone, her hair flowed down her back and glowed in the low colored lights, and her body appeared slender in a pair of slim, black pants and a snug lace blouse. Katy herself wore a long black skirt and a lacy top as well. She went over to the piano and sat down while Jayne tested the microphone.

Laura sat at their table giving them a thumbs-up sign.

Katy played a few riffs. She understood Jayne's love of the music world.

Then she saw Adam come in and sit down beside his sister.

Laura said something to him and Adam sat hunched at the table, reminding Katy of the time he had come to the restaurant to meet her and return her earrings. Falling in love had seemed so long ago now. What had happened to that love? Love needed to be nurtured, not shunned as Adam seemed to be doing.

Jayne turned to her, Katy began to play, Jayne began to sing, and the first musical night at Veggie Things began.

•

Adam watched his daughter while his wife's music filled the small restaurant. Standing with the spotlight on her, holding the microphone, Jayne appeared very much in control. She thanked everyone for coming, especially Katy Kerr Stevenson whose songs she was going to sing. "A wonderful new talent," Jayne said.

He had asked for this, Adam thought as Jayne sang to Katy's accompaniment. He had placed Jayne and Katy together in the house. He had left them alone. They had developed music together. He could have stopped it.

But why?

The song Jayne sang was wonderfully poignant. Katy was way more talented than he'd ever expected. And Jayne's talent brought tears to his eyes. She was more polished than her mother had ever been, which was needed in today's music climate. She had the chance to be big. And he should help her. After all, she was his daughter, his flesh and blood. He'd only denied her because of his fear of losing her.

But now he knew the inevitable, what his family had been telling him for years, he would lose far more of her if he didn't let her go and do what her heart demanded. Even if she failed she wouldn't be able to blame the failure on him.

Besides, he had Katy now. He had someone who cared.

The small venue went mad with applause after Jayne's first performance. "And now my second song, also by Katy, *Those Expectations*."

The song started off with a slow melody and lyrics that spoke of the expectations a woman always had when she went into a relationship. Adam was stunned by the melody and lyrics. Sung by Jayne, whose voice was mature beyond her years, he felt his heart contract. Then the music quickened and Jayne sang angrily of those expectations never being met. He was so enthralled he thought like a businessman. He might have a female Elton John and Bernie Taupin, a singer-song-writer duo.

When they finished, they came over to him and he stood up and looked at his daughter, the woman, not the little girl.

She turned away to wipe away surreptitious tears before she went into his arms. "Thanks for coming."

"You were great. No, more than great," he told her, holding her tight. "You're fantastic. And I was a fool. I'll definitely help," he said as they pulled apart.

He turned to Katy. "You're great as well. Thank you."

"Thank you for the idea to have entertainment at my restaurant."

Laura rose and picked up her purse. "Jayne's staying with a friend tonight. I'll take her home," she said.

When his sister was on her way with Jayne, Adam said to Katy, "So are you going home now?"

"No," Katy said, not looking at him. "Heather and Joe have a new house. I'm staying there."

He felt his heart contract. What an idiot he'd been. "Are you moving out on me?" The words came out strained and desperate. His heart screamed, *Don't leave me Katy. You can't leave me.* But he didn't actually say the words. He couldn't. Because when he did, he would become extremely vulnerable. He saw her throat move as she picked up her black blazer.

"I think it's best for a while," she said.

*Vulnerable be damned*, he thought. He was hurting so badly now, what did it matter? "Katy. Reconsider what you're about to do."

She shouldered her purse. "Adam. We can't discuss this here." She walked out of the restaurant and stood on the sidewalk.

He followed her. "Then come home with me and we'll talk."

"Only if you're ready?"

Adam let out a breath and the words came out. "I am ready. I love you, Katy. Please believe me. Give me a chance. I'll give our marriage a chance. I know how you feel. You told it all in your song, but I want to meet those expectations for you. I want to be the one."

He saw her eyes close for a moment. "I don't know, Adam. I really don't know. I haven't been feeling much lately. I'm not sure if I'm up to a big scene tonight. I'm not sure if I'm ready for a decision yet."

"Then we won't talk tonight. We'll talk tomorrow. But we can be in the same house."

"You don't have to go away?"

"No. I'm free for about a month now. Besides, Tom's heart attack scared me."

"You mean, you're going to slow down?" she asked.

He nodded. "Yes." He reached for her hand. Then he walked with Katy to his car.

•

Katy followed Adam into the room where she'd first acquainted herself with him. Tonight rain pattered against the French windows and she could see nothing of the garden.

"Jayne was great," she said.

"Fantastic." He gave her a lopsided smile. "I blame myself for everything, Katy. I've been so cruel to Jayne. And all because of my own fear and insecurity. And your songs. I mean, you're great."

"Jayne's a wonderful vehicle for my work."

"You're right. I didn't know she could do that angry

rock stuff. I'm going to make sure that both of you get the recognition you deserve."

"You're not worried anymore about the media and comparisons with Rachel and Jayne anymore?"

"She'll have to deal with it, won't she? If that's what she wants. But I didn't think she sounded like her mother tonight. She seemed very much to have her own style. Besides, there is a generation or two out there who probably don't remember Rachel anyway."

Katy smiled slightly. "Probably. Whatever happens I believe she's strong enough to survive. You brought her up well, Adam. You can't deny yourself that pat on the back."

"I was proud of her tonight."

"That's all she wants."

"And now let's get on with us," Adam said. "I want to clear up everything tonight, while we have no one here to bother us."

"You think we can clear everything up in a moment, don't you?" Katy told him. "I'm not a performer wanting a contract that can be negotiated with a few pen strikes here and there. I'm your wife, Adam. I love you. I'm trying to understand if you love me or not and if you can let me see that love once in a while, other than in bed. Sex is sex. When it's over it's easy to withdraw from one another."

He smiled. "You've always been so forthright."

"Honest, Adam. Because I don't like being hurt. I don't deal with hurt very well. I like to get on with my life and enjoy it."

"That's not always possible."

"I know. But we have to grab the best we can. We're both young, we have careers that converge. But I want more than that, Adam. I would like a real loving life with you."

"It means I have to make some changes."

"If that's what it means, yes," she said. "You're the boss. You can hire people to do work for you."

"You want me to do that?"

"I want you to do what you want to do. If you don't want to come to me and meet me half way, then I have to go, because I can't be married to a man who isn't my best friend."

She saw his shoulders stiffen.

"I'm here. I've accommodated my life to fit yours. Now you have to accommodate your life to fit mine, so that we become more of a unit."

"I will still have to go away occasionally."

"That's fine. I can deal with an occasional absence. I have a lot of work on my plate right now. I will probably have to exclude you from my life some of the time. But not all of the time. I can't be used for sex between visits. I told you that right from the beginning."

"You've never been that, Katy. I loved you from the beginning. I opened that door and you were the woman I wanted."

"Then keep me by loving me and showing me you love me by being with me."

He lifted her chin and pressed his mouth to her cheeks and kissed away her tears. "When Tom got sick I realized that I wasn't off the hook myself. I could easily head in that direction. I don't want to lose my life, my physical freedom, my wife … Katy, I love you. You've made me feel again."

"And you're not frightened of that love?"

"Yes. I'm frightened."

"Good." She smiled through her tears. "Because I'm frightened as well, but it's a good fear. It makes me want to cling to you all the time."

"Then cling."

They went up to bed and made love slowly and awoke in the morning to a silent house. Adam climbed out of bed and picked up his cell phone.

"What are you doing?" Katy asked with her elbow lifting her off the pillow. Seeing Adam with the phone made her stomach suddenly coil into a knot again. Why had she succumbed to him last night? Why hadn't she stuck to her guns and left him?

"Turning the damn thing off. I think I'm going to stop carrying it around from now on."

Relief made Katy laugh with tears in her eyes. "When did you decide this?"

He crawled back into bed with her and pressed his finger down her damp cheek to the edge of her mouth. "After I met you at the door that weekend, I came upstairs and I was thinking about you like some kid let out of school for the summer. That phone rang and I wanted to smash it. I didn't want it anymore."

She kissed his finger. "But you went back to it."

"Because that's how my life was. We can re-organize SMM. We'll do what you suggest. Hire more staff. Whatever it takes."

"But we'll still have a lot of music in our life?"

"Damn right. You're a talent to be reckoned with. And I'm sure Jayne will keep us busy with her career. And there might be more children?"

Katy smiled. "There might be, but not until I know for sure the child will have a full-time father."

"I promise," Adam said.

"And I'm to believe that?"

"How can I make you believe me?"

"Be here for me as much as possible, Adam. Include me. Show me."

"I love you, Katy. Everything that has gone before me in my life is now overshadowed by you. But I just couldn't quite grasp how much you actually meant to me."

She stroked his hair back from his forehead. "You only wanted happiness. I understand. I was making it rough for you, I suppose."

"No. You made me see sense. And you helped me release Jayne. You've made me live again, Katy. You have to stick by me. I need you."

"I need you too, though, Adam."

"And I have to remember that." He kissed her mouth softly. "I will remember that. And if I forget, please remind me. You can be quite forceful, so don't hold back."

Katy laughed. "I never held back with you, did I?"

"No." His hands slid down her body. "And I'm pleased you didn't."

Katy buried her head against his warm shoulder. "The thought of not having you scares me."

His arms tightened. "The way not having you scares me."

"I'm so pleased you're scared."

"That's nice of you."

They both laughed and began to kiss, the kiss gradually warming to lovemaking. Her expectations, for once, were met.

• • •

# Jillian Dagg

Jillian Dagg was born in Surrey, England, and moved to Canada with her parents. She loved reading romance novels so much that she began writing the genre. Her first books were published by Silhouette, Simon & Schuster and a writing career was launched. Jillian lives in Ontario, Canada with her husband and cats.

**www.jilliandagg.com**

---

## You might also enjoy:

A whirlwind of lust and energy, famous composer Eric Ries offers up seduction and excitement until Jenna's passion for music is thoroughly entwined with her obsession for him. In Josh Kendal, she catches a glimpse of depth and sincerity—and is torn between the temptations that have shaped her life and the kind of love she's never had.

www.ingramcontent.com/pod-product-compliance
Lightning Source LLC
Chambersburg PA
CBHW071426260626
47170CB00008B/2610